Gideon
Johann

By
Duane Boehm

Gideon Johann

For more information or permission contact: boehmduane@gmail.com

This book is a work of fiction. References to real people, events, establishments, organizations, or locales are intended only to provide a sense of authenticity and are used fictitiously. All other characters, and all incidents and dialogue are drawn from the author's imagination and not to be construed as real.

ISBN: 1-71734-896-3

Other Books by Duane Boehm

In Just One Moment
Last Stand: A Gideon Johann Western Book 1
Last Chance: A Gideon Johann Western Book 2
Last Hope: A Gideon Johann Western Book 3
Last Ride: A Gideon Johann Western Book 4
Last Breath: A Gideon Johann Western Book 5
Last Journey: A Gideon Johann Western Book 6
Last Atonement: A Gideon Johann Western Book 7
Where The Wild Horses Roam: Wild Horse Westerns Book 1
Spirit Of The Wild Horse: Wild Horse Westerns Book 2
Wanted: A Collection of Western Stories (7 authors)
Wanted II: A Collection of Western Stories (7 authors)

Dedicated to Aunt Virginia and her love of books

Chapter 1

On a cool summer night, Gideon Johann and Farting Jack Dolan ambled out of the Royal Flush Saloon at just after midnight. Both men staggered a little as they stepped off the boardwalk into the street. They had spent the evening sipping whiskey and playing cards. With Gideon's winnings, he had succeeded in doubling his initial stake while Jack had managed just to break even after finally finding a little luck with the last couple of hands of poker. Jack mounted his horse to head for his shack on the edge of Boulder while Gideon crossed the street toward the boardinghouse where he lived.

"Don't fall off your horse and break your neck, you old coot," Gideon called out.

Jack lifted his ass off the saddle and retorted with a resounding fart. "Whoa, that was a good one," he remarked more to himself than Gideon.

When Gideon entered the house, the sound of the creaking front door carried to the bedroom of Mrs. Stewart, the widow proprietor, alerting her that he had returned home. She didn't take kindly to her boarders coming in so late, but since Gideon was a town deputy, and because Sheriff Howell had personally vouched for the young man, she didn't see much choice but to bite her lip and let him come and go as he pleased. She always made a point to be aloof the next morning at breakfast, but if Gideon ever noticed, he certainly never took the hint.

As Gideon walked through the dark house, he bumped into a table and had to make a quick grab of the oil lamp sitting there to prevent the light from crashing to the floor. He stumbled to his room, pulled off his clothes, and dropped into the bed, staring up into the dark ceiling.

Most nights, the alcohol chased his terrifying visions away, but he had a bad feeling about tonight. He fought off closing his eyes for as long as he could, but weariness began to set in and his lids sank shut. The little dead boy with the vacant stare immediately gazed back at him. Gideon bolted up in the bed and slammed his fists into the mattress. The little boy had been haunting him since near the end of the War Between the States when Gideon had helplessly watched the child die. Sometimes Gideon wondered if the boy's soul had crawled into him on that dreaded day. The vision had been getting progressively worse for some time now, and the only thing that would chase it from his mind was to move away. He would have left Boulder a long time ago except for his loyalty to Sheriff Howell and his friendship with Farting Jack. The little boy would always find him again, but with a little luck, Gideon would give him the slip for a good while.

Widow Stewart didn't allow alcohol in her house, but Gideon kept whiskey in his nightstand anyway. He pulled the bottle from the drawer and took a long guzzle before dropping back onto his pillow. The room felt like as if it were spinning now, but he was so drunk that he passed out into a dreamless sleep.

In the morning, Gideon woke with his head pounding and his mouth so dry that he could barely swallow. The whiskey bottle on the nightstand looked tempting just to wet his throat, but he couldn't quite bring himself to take a drink first thing in the morning. He willed himself out of bed to get dressed. As he stepped into the hall, the smell of eggs cooking and bacon frying overwhelmed his senses and he started retching. Gideon made a dash outside and stood on the porch bent over with his hands braced on his knees for support as he gagged. He sucked in big breaths of air until the nausea passed.

Farting Jack rode up to the boardinghouse. "You look like hell warmed over."

"Thanks. That's just what I wanted to hear first thing this morning. What are you doing in town?" Gideon asked.

"The sheriff said he'd have my money today for when I helped him track down that horse thief," Jack replied.

Jack led the life of a mountain man that supplemented his income from trapping with work for the sheriff when the lawman needed a tracker. The sheriff considered Jack the best white man scout in the territory. When winter came, Jack headed into the mountains to trap. Some years, he'd never see another person until springtime when he'd return with his pelts.

"Good. I can kill two birds with one stone."

Jack raised his eyebrows and pursed his lips, but didn't ask what Gideon meant. He nudged his horse into moving, following Gideon as the deputy walked toward the jail. The two men walked into the sheriff's office together, finding Sheriff Howell sitting at his desk drinking coffee and perusing wanted posters.

Looking up, Sheriff Howell raked his finger across his mustache before saying, "Well, I didn't find either of your pictures in this stack of posters, but the way you two look this morning, I'm not sure I'd recognize you anyway." He picked up an envelope and held it out for Jack to take.

Jack grabbed his money and said, "We could be on a poster before the day is out for killing a surly sheriff."

The sheriff grinned. "Good morning to you, too."

Gideon dropped into a chair and let out a loud breath. "Sheriff, I can't stay in Boulder any longer. I quit."

The sheriff had heard the same story from Gideon a couple of time before, and took the news with a grain of salt. "You can't leave. Boulder is your home now. Everybody likes you here."

"I mean it this time. I like working for you just fine, but it's past my time to move on. I can't help it – I really can't."

Sheriff Howell sat back in his chair, let out a sigh, and used his thumb and his middle finger to stroke both sides of his mustache. Gideon's tone was beginning to make him think that the young man meant what he said this time. "You're going to leave me mighty short-handed. Deputies like you don't come along every day."

"I appreciate that. You have no idea how much I wish I could stay," Gideon said as he began rubbing the one-inch vertical scar on his cheekbone.

Farting Jack tugged on his long beard. "Are you headed back to Cheyenne to work on the Big Dipper Ranch again?"

"No, I've never backtracked yet. I don't plan to start now," Gideon said and then smiled. "And besides, there's a whore there that wanted to marry me. I think I'll head to Ellsworth, Kansas and try to join up with a cattle crew headed back to Texas – see what that's like down there."

The sheriff stood and walked around his desk until he stopped in front of Gideon's chair. "Son, I don't know what ghost you have chasing you, and God knows that Jack and I have tried to get you to talk about it, but no one ever outruns their past. The only choice a man has is to accept it and move on. We all have things we'd like to change, but life doesn't work that way."

Gideon removed his hat and ran his hand through his thatch of unruly hair. "I wish I could. Maybe the problem is that I'm just not man enough."

Jack took a seat beside Gideon and looked into his friend's troubled face. He'd seen this day coming for quite a while. Gideon's drinking had gotten progressively worse, and the young man had been sullen and restless for a few weeks. He'd also lost weight from his already thin frame. The old mountain man had grown fond of the deputy and worried about his well-being. He also feared Gideon would get himself into trouble out on his own. "My brother lives in Ellsworth. I think I'll ride with you and pay him a visit. I can keep you company."

Surprised by Jack's plan, Gideon said, "That's the first I've ever heard of you having a brother. And who says I want company? I've managed on my own for a long time. I certainly don't need some old farting mountain man babysitting me."

"Well, unless you plan on shooting me, I don't see that there's much you can do to stop me. And seeing how you once saved my life, I don't think you're going to be doing that," Jack replied.

The first time that Jack met Gideon, he had been leery of the young buck. To his way of thinking, the new deputy seemed way too brash and disrespectful. Jack had accompanied the sheriff, a deputy, and Gideon as they set out to find a couple of killers. The outlaws ambushed the law party and Jack had taken a bullet. As Jack lay on the side of a steep hill with little cover for protection, the criminals tried to kill him. Gideon, realizing that Jack was in dire straits, had charged his horse straight into the gunfire, killing the two bandits. After that, Jack decided that Gideon's personality suited him just fine.

Grinning, Gideon said, "I guess saving you is another regret I'll carry around for the rest of my life." He stood and pulled his badge from his shirt. Gazing at the silver star, a rush of sadness washed over him like a wave. He guessed he'd never get to stick to any job that he really liked.

The sheriff turned toward Jack. "How am I supposed to get by with my best deputy and my only tracker both gone?"

"You managed before and you'll manage now. I'll be back in a month or so. You need to pay me more if I'm that valuable," Jack said.

Ignoring Jack, Sheriff Howell took the badge from Gideon, and shook his hand. "Gideon, you take care of yourself. There'll always be a job waiting here if you ever want it."

"Thank you, sir. I appreciate all you've done for me. You and Jack have taught me a lot about being a lawman and a tracker," Gideon said as he plopped his hat onto his head.

Jack arose from his chair. "I'll head home to pack and then I'll meet you in front of the boardinghouse."

"Yes, by all means," Gideon said. "If I didn't know better, I'd think you were sweet on me and couldn't stand for us to be apart."

Chapter 2

The traveling toward Ellsworth made for easy riding. After crossing the foothills outside of Boulder, Gideon and Jack rode through Denver before heading into the plains on their trip to reach Kansas.

As the two men broke camp on the sixth morning of their journey, Jack remarked, "Have you ever seen so much flatland in all your life? I can't imagine why anybody would want to live out here, and that's saying something since I grew up on land like this. A man needs to see some mountains every morning so he stays humble."

Gideon smiled, feeling better than he had in weeks. He'd only had trouble getting to sleep on the first night out of Boulder. Since then, he'd slept like a baby. "I've seen all this kind of land before during the war. We were all over Kansas, Missouri, and Arkansas. And you're right that this is some mighty flat land. We can see anybody coming from a long ways away. I figure we crossed into Kansas last night just before we made camp," he said as he emptied the coffee pot onto the campfire.

"I'm not sure I want to see my brother bad enough to suffer this ride. A man can't get his bearings out here. It all looks the same."

"Well, it's not as if I asked you along for the trip. You invited yourself."

"Saddle your horse and let's ride. You talk too much," Jack responded.

They had ridden a couple of hours, when to the east, Gideon spotted a plume of smoke. "I wonder what's causing that."

"Fire would be my guess," Jack replied.

Gideon shook his head in exasperation before nudging his horse into a fast trot. As they neared the flames, the remnants of a burned-out covered wagon came into view. A man, woman, and a young boy were sprawled out in grotesque fashion nearby. They had all been shot multiple times and scalped. Turkey buzzards surrounded the woman and pecked at her corpse without fear of the approaching men. Jack drew his revolver and fired into the birds, killing one as the others scattered. When Gideon caught sight of the boy, he had to jump from his horse to keep from vomiting on its neck. He fell down to his knees as his breakfast shot from his stomach. After that, dry heaves gripped him until he swore that at any moment his innards were going to come flying out of his mouth.

Jack walked around observing the site as he waited for Gideon to regain his composure. Gideon finally got to his feet and tried to clear his head with some deep breaths. Embarrassed by his actions, he avoided Jack as he scouted for tracks.

"I'll track these Indians to hell and back if I have to, and kill every last one of them," Gideon swore.

Shaking his head, Jack gave Gideon a look that a disappointed parent would give their misguided child. "I've spent a lot of time teaching you how to look for signs, and you've become a right fine tracker, but you're seeing what these murderers want you to see instead of the truth."

Gideon furrowed his brow and squeezed his lips tightly together. He glanced around the area one more time. "I did notice there were only three sets of hoof prints. I thought Indian war parties traveled in bigger groups than that."

"That's a fair point. Keep looking."

Strolling about, Gideon studied the tracks once more. "The horses are shod."

"Never seen an Indian with a shooed horse, have you?"

"I can't believe I missed that. You've taught me better than that."

"You were upset and not thinking clearly. Just remember next time to look for what's there and not what you think is going to be there," Jack said.

"I still plan to go find them. Nobody is going to get away with this if I can help it. They can't be that far away. That family was cooking breakfast this morning when they were attacked. I doubt the killers figured on anybody finding the bodies this soon. Those poor people probably had ten dollars to their name and they had to die for it," Gideon said.

"Gideon, you're not the law anymore and we're a long way from home. We need to find the next town and report this to the law."

"You can head on toward Ellsworth. I'll meet up with you there. There's no way I'm not going after these butchers," Gideon said before spitting to get the taste of bile from his mouth.

"I'm not leaving you. We'll do this together. I saw a shovel by the wagon. The handle looked only charred a little. We need to bury these folks before we do anything else. I'll be damned if I let the buzzards and wolves have them," Jack said before walking away toward the remains of the wagon.

By the time they dug the holes and buried the bodies, it was nearing noon. With no appetite for food after such a gruesome morning, they rode out in a lope following the tracks to the southeast.

"How could anybody be so gruel as to kill a child and scalp him?" Gideon mused.

"You know as well as I do that some people are just pure evil. They're capable of any act of barbarism. It's always been that way and I expect it always will be," Jack said.

"Well, there will be three less of them when I'm done."

After riding a few miles, Jack noticed something bright red off to the side of the trail. He pointed for Gideon to see before turning his horse toward it. The three scalps were stuck together lying in the grass, covered with flies.

"I suppose they figured varmints would drag the scalps away before anybody found them," Jack said.

"What are we going to do with them?" Gideon asked as he felt his stomach start churning again.

"I guess leave them. We don't have a way to dig a hole and I'm sure not going to take them with me."

"I wish we had time to burn them, but we've lost enough ground burying the family," Gideon said as he nudged his horse into moving. The sight of the boy still lingered in his mind along with the smell of death. He didn't wish to stay any longer viewing the scalps.

The men rode on through the rest of day, pushing their horses as hard as they dared well into dusk.

"We have to stop. I'm as good of a tracker as you'll ever find, but I ain't no owl. We're liable to veer off the trail if we go on any farther. I don't want to waste time trying to find their tracks again in the morning," Jack said.

"I suppose. Do you think we made up much ground?" Gideon asked.

"Oh, we made up a lot of ground. They're not that far ahead of us. We'll ride out at first light in the morning, and I think we'll catch them before noon," Jack replied.

"I sure hope so."

After making camp and eating a meal of jerky and hardtack, Gideon pulled a whiskey bottle from his saddlebag. He held the bottle up to the light of the fire and studied it for a moment before taking a long, slow drink. As he wiped his mouth on his sleeve, he held out the bottle to his friend.

Jack waved off the bottle. "Not tonight. I guess I'm not in the mood," he said.

Before taking another drink, Gideon asked, "Do you think there's really a Hell for people like the ones we're chasing?"

The mountain man's eyes got big as he tugged on his beard. The question perplexed him. He and Gideon had never had such conversations before, and Jack wasn't sure he wanted to start now. "I never had a Christian upbringing so I'm probably not the one to ask such a deep question, but I have to think there's a special place for those people. I do know that people have souls – at least most of them do. So maybe that means there is a Hell for them."

Gideon let out a little chuckle. "I don't know why I give a damn. I probably should be more worried that I'll be down there with those sons of bitches."

Jack picked up a stick and stirred some ashes as he stared at the fire. "I don't know why you're so hard on yourself. If you believe in Hell, you have to believe in Heaven and forgiveness, too. I think you've been forgiven for your sins – you just need to forgive yourself."

"Jack, you have no idea. Some things are just unforgiveable – even accidents."

Tossing the stick into the flames, Jack said, "You wouldn't talk about this stuff if you didn't want your life to change. You just need the courage to do it. It's easier for you to go on as you are rather than change and be happy."

Picking the bottle up from off the ground, Gideon took a big swig. As the minutes passed, he stared at the fire. Finally, he said, "How do you know that people have souls?"

Looking around as if he were planning his escape, Jack began pulling on his beard again and mumbling under his breath. "If you laugh at me, I swear I'll shoot you where you sit. I can sense the color of a person's soul. It kind of surrounds them."

Gideon felt too astounded by the admission to think of laughing. He gazed at Jack with a blank expression. "What color is mine?" he asked meekly.

"Yours changes all the time, but on a good day, it's a color I see on real good folks. That's all I have to say on the matter," Jack said before leaning over and grabbing the whiskey. He took a long drink before returning the bottle to the ground.

"You can actually see a color surrounding a person?"

Jack let out a loud sigh, sorry he had confessed his special talent. "I don't know that I would go that far, but I just get a perception of a color from a person."

"I think I'm turning in on that note. It's been a long day," Gideon said before crawling into his bedroll. He didn't feel like talking any longer and had no idea where to take the conversation anyway after Jack's startling revelation.

Gideon closed his eyes knowing that the vision of the dead boy with the staring eyes would be haunting him that night. Seeing the other boy's mutilated body had been too much for him and left his emotions raw. Hours passed as he listened to Jack's snoring before he finally dozed off into a good sleep.

Jack shook Gideon awake when the sky to the east showed only the faintest sign of light. Gideon could barely open his eyes and looked up at Jack in confusion for a moment before coming to his senses. He got to his feet and stumbled to the edge of the camp to take a piss.

After grabbing up some wood they'd gathered the previous night, Jack got the campfire blazing. He retrieved the coffee pot and skillet, and started making coffee and frying bacon as Gideon saddled the horses. The men ate their breakfast in silence. By the time they were ready to ride, the sun had peeked up over the horizon just enough to follow the trail.

Once the horses' muscles were warmed, they put the animals into a lope and held the pace for an hour. As they topped a hill, a tree-lined creek came into view. Gideon suddenly held up his hand.

"I caught a whiff of smoke," Gideon said as he reached back into his saddlebag and pulled out his spyglass. He studied the woods.

"I smell it, too," Jack said.

"I can see the slightest hint of smoke rising over that way," Gideon said as he pointed toward the spot. "There's too much cover to see anything else. Let's get out of sight."

They turned the horses and retreated to the bottom of the hill.

"We can follow this hill around and then make an arc until we hit the creek. With a little luck, they won't see us and we can come up the creek and surprise them. What do you think?" Jack said.

"It beats charging them. You think it has to be them, don't you?"

"Yeah, it's them. The tracks were headed right to that spot where you pointed."

After following the base of the hill, they trotted in a semicircle to the creek. The woods along the stream were too thick to maneuver the horses through without making all kinds of racket. They tied their mounts to saplings and retrieved their rifles. Gideon took the lead as they made their way upstream. They had walked a couple hundred yards when the sound of voices carried to them.

Jack motioned that he planned to cross the creek so that they could cover the outlaws from different directions. Gideon watched Jack slip across the stream. The agility of the old man amazed him. He hoped he aged as well as his friend. They resumed walking until they caught sight of three men eating breakfast in a little clearing. Gideon glanced over at Jack and saw the mountain man give a thumb up sign that he was ready.

After raising his rifle and taking aim, Gideon yelled, "We have you surrounded. Stand up and put your hands in the air."

The three outlaws jumped up and attempted to scatter in different directions. Gideon squeezed off a shot and thought he hit his mark though the man kept on moving. Jack fired a round, and his man hit the ground, but jumped up and scampered for cover.

"Give up or we're going to shoot you to pieces," Gideon hollered.

Gideon's remark was answered with a wild shot that came nowhere near him. One of the outlaws made a break for the horses. Gideon took aim and fired his rifle. The man jumped up in the air as if he were a rabbit, grabbing his hip in midair before falling to the ground. The two remaining murderers unleashed a barrage of shots in the direction from where they had heard Gideon's voice. Gideon's return fire forced one of the men to move to a spot that gave Jack a clear shot. Jack took quick aim and fired. The outlaw grabbed his chest and flopped over onto the ground.

"We surrender," a voice called out.

"All of you stand up where I can see you and put your hands in the air," Gideon bellowed.

"I believe Smitty is dead, and Roscoe is shot in the ass. I don't think he can stand," the outlaw said as he stood and put his arms above his head. Blood streamed down his left arm.

As Gideon and Jack cautiously walked into camp, they kept a watchful eye on the outlaws. The three men looked as if they had been used for target practice. The one that had done the talking had been hit in the arm with Jack's first shot. The one named Smitty had died from Jack's shot to the chest. He also had a leg wound from Gideon's initial round of fire. Roscoe was moaning and clutching his butt cheek.

"What's your name?" Gideon asked.

"People call me Butch."

"That was a cruel thing that you did to that family," Gideon remarked before reloading his rifle.

Butch looked down at the ground and didn't speak again.

Jack retrieved some leather strips from the pouch he wore around his neck on a rawhide strap and tied the men's hands behind their backs.

"What are we going to do with them now?" Jack asked.

"Hang them. I meant what I said," Gideon answered.

Butch's eyes grew as large as half-dollars. He spun around and took off running. Gideon and Jack drew their revolvers and fired simultaneously. Both shots smacked into the back of Butch's skull. A junk of scalp flew through the air in a mist of blood and brains.

"Just shoot me, too. I don't want to hang," Roscoe cried out.

"Did you give that family a choice on how they wanted to die or if they wanted to keep their scalps?" Gideon asked as he retrieved a lasso from a saddle on the ground.

Gideon made a hangman's noose and then found a tree branch to his liking. He threw the rope over it while Jack saddled one of the outlaw's horses. By that time, Roscoe was crying and begging for mercy as Gideon and Jack hoisted him up onto the saddle. As

Gideon slipped the noose over Roscoe's head, guilt started creeping into his conscience for what he was about to do. He quickly slapped the horse on the rump before he had the chance to change his mind. The horse bolted and Roscoe's neck snapped with a crack, killing him instantly.

"You have a nasty streak in you," Jack said as he watched Roscoe swinging from the rope.

Glancing toward the body, Gideon felt hollow. Serving up justice had brought no sense of righting a wrong. "No, I have a revengeful streak. There's a difference," Gideon replied.

"Maybe so, but I hope I'm never on the receiving end of your wrath either way."

"I don't know why you'd say that – I am loyal and you know that. Let's get our horses and get out of here. I want to forget all this," Gideon said.

"You certainly keep life interesting. I'll give you that," Jack said as he picked up his rifle.

Chapter 3

Jack grinned as if he'd won a prize when he read the sign that announced that the town coming into view was Ellsworth, Kansas. "Thank God, we're finally here. I'm so tired of riding this horse. My ass has got to have calluses on it. To show you what a fine friend I am, I'm going to buy you a beer in the first saloon we come upon."

"Sounds good to me."

Ellsworth looked to be a bustling town even though the livestock pens were empty and the cowboys from the cattle drives had yet to arrive from the south. Men dressed in everything from suits to not much more than rags were loitering on the boardwalks. Scantily clad whores as well as women dressed in their Sunday best were out on the street shopping. A couple of prostitutes sat on the balcony of a saloon, smoking cigarettes and laughing.

"Don't look much like Boulder," Jack said with a chuckle.

"No, it doesn't. I think a man could get himself into trouble around here," Gideon said as he stopped his horse in front of the first saloon they spotted.

Gideon and Jack climbed down from their horses and walked stiff-legged into the Red Rose Saloon. The place looked dark and dingy with smoke hovering at the ceiling. A crowd of afternoon drinkers took note of the newly arrived strangers, but offered no welcome. A gambler in a black suit and string tie sat at a table relentlessly shuffling a deck of cards while waiting for a game. He passed the time sipping whiskey and laughing with the whore keeping him company.

"Bartender, we'll have two beers, if you please," Jack said as he sidled up to the bar.

The bartender gave Jack the once-over, but made no comment as he dabbed the perspiration from his head with a bar rag. His dirty blond hair was so soaked in pomade that it gave the appearance of being drenched in sweat. He poured the beers and set the mugs down roughly. "Twenty-five cents," he said in a croaky voice.

Jack reached into his pocket and paid the tab. He took his first drink and smacked his lips a couple of times. "That's pretty good beer," he said to Gideon.

"Not bad. I've certainly had worse," Gideon replied.

The gambler shooed the whore away. "Would you two gentlemen like to join me in a game of cards?" he called out.

Turning to face the voice, Jack said, "No thanks. We've been in the saddle for days and the last thing I want to do right now is sit in a hard old chair."

"What's the matter, grandpa? Are you afraid you'll lose that buckskin outfit to me? We've got Indians around here where you could always go steal another one," the gambler chided.

Jack laughed and turned his head to get a glance at Gideon. He could see the veins already bulging in his friend's neck, so he gave him a wink in the hopes of calming him down.

"Why don't you tell me a story, grandpa?" the gambler called out.

Having to turn his attention back to the gambler, Jack asked, "What's your name?"

"Burton Rochester, if it's any of your concern."

"Well, Burton, here's my story. I was taking money from the likes of you back when your momma was still turning you over her knee and trying to spank some manners into you. I might have to do the same if you don't watch your tongue."

The comment caused the bar patrons to explode with laughter. Burton Rochester turned red. He jumped up from his chair and came marching toward Jack. Gideon had seen many a gambler carry a concealed Derringer in their sleeve. When Rochester started to swing up his arm, Gideon reacted. He grabbed the gambler by the wrist, and in the same motion, drove his knee into Burton's groin. The gambler dropped to the floor as if the bones in his legs had turned to mush. With catlike reflexes, Gideon pulled his knife from its sheath and sliced open Rochester's suit coat and shirt, exposing the Derringer. He retrieved the gun and set it on the bar before yanking the gambler to his feet. After grabbing Burton by the belt and suit collar, Gideon took off running and threw the gambler out into the street. All eyes were upon him when he walked back into the saloon. He stared back waiting for the next challenge, but Jack grabbed Gideon's arm and pulled him to the bar.

"I could have handled myself just fine. You need to calm down. We don't need to make a ruckus on our first day in town," Jack admonished.

"He was going to shoot you," Gideon said in bewilderment.

"You don't know that."

"The hell I don't. He swung his arm up so that his Derringer would pop out of his sleeve. I've seen it done in the past."

"Maybe so, but it doesn't mean he would have fired it. I guess it was better to stop him than find out too late what his intentions were, but I imagine he was just trying to save face," Jack said in hopes of pacifying his friend.

Gideon didn't reply, but took a drink from his mug instead.

The bartender walked over with two more beers and actually smiled, showing off his big square teeth. "These are on the house. You boys made my day considerably brighter. This here is my place and I get tired of that gambler's mouth, too. I'm Edward Calhoun, but you can call me Teddy." The saloonkeeper wiped his hand on his apron before shaking Gideon and Jack's hands.

Halfway through his second beer, Gideon's mood started to improve. He grinned and looked over at Jack. "That was a pretty clever line you used on that gambler," he said.

Jack winked and nodded his head. "I'm a pretty clever fellow," he said before belly laughing. He tipped up his glass and drained the remainder of his beer. "Let's go find a general store. I need some pipe tobacco. I ran out three days ago, and I have a real hankering for a smoke."

They walked down the main street of Ellsworth until spotting McIntire's General Store. As they stepped up to the entrance, a woman's voice, just short of yelling, could be heard coming from inside of the business. Gideon looked at Jack, and the mountain man shrugged before opening the door. Inside a tall, slender young woman with auburn hair stood behind the counter with her hands resting on her hips in a pose of determination. Even with the scowl on her face, she looked pretty with big brown eyes and full lips. Three men stood at the counter with their arms full of supplies. They wore side arms and dressed as if they were more than likely ranchers.

"Willis, you haven't paid your tab in over a year. At some point, it just becomes charity. We are trying to make a living here, too," the woman lectured.

"Chloe, we'll have cattle to sell this fall. I'll pay you then."

"No, you've reached your limit. I mean it this time," Chloe insisted.

"You'll get your damned money. Put all this on my tab. Your pa should keep you at home where you belong," Willis said, turning and walking toward the door.

Gideon blocked the exit. "Mister, the lady said no," he said.

"Who the hell are you?"

"I'm the man that's going to stop you from leaving with those goods."

Willis dropped the supplies to the floor, but before he succeeded in reaching for his revolver, Gideon sent a right hook crashing into his jaw. The punch sent Willis flying into a shelf, nearly toppling it.

Jack drew his revolver and trained it on the other two men before they had a chance to go for their guns. "You boys need to keep your hands full of those supplies. I got a twitchy finger."

Willis recovered quickly and charged Gideon, knocking him up against the counter and pinning his arms against his sides. Gideon head-butted Willis across the bridge of the nose. With a loud groan, Willis grabbed his face, enabling Gideon to deliver a left and right into his foe's stomach. The blows doubled over Willis. As he gasped for air, Gideon dispensed a windmill punch to the jaw. Willis flew backwards into the shelf again, knocking it over this time and sending goods crashing and breaking. He slid to the floor and didn't move.

"Take your friend and get out of here," Jack ordered.

The two men set their supplies on the counter before lifting Willis up by the arms and dragging him out of the store.

Gideon glanced over at Chloe. Her face looked as red as if she were holding her breath and contorted in anger that concealed the beauty Gideon had admired when he entered the store. She walked around the counter to get a better view of the damages.

"I don't know who you are or what you think you're doing, but you probably just cost me more money than if I had given away everything they were carrying. I'll be cleaning this mess up all day," Chloe yelled.

"My name's Gideon Johann. I'll pay for the damages and help you clean up the place."

"I don't want your money or your help. Just get out of here."

"I insist," Gideon said in his no-nonsense way, rubbing the scar on his cheek as was his habit when agitated or in deep thought.

Jack stepped forward so that he stood between Gideon and Chloe.

"Ma'am, let me introduce myself. I'm Jack Dolan," he said before making a slight bow and giving his friendliest smile. "My friend here is a little overzealous in his chivalry, but I assure you that his intentions were well-meant and honorable. Please let us assist you in cleaning this up and paying you for the damages. It is the least we could do for the trouble we have caused you."

Chloe smiled in spite of herself. Jack's charisma had done the trick in squashing her resolve to evict the men.

"If you insist," Chloe said.

As Chloe went to the back of the store to retrieve a broom, Gideon and Jack righted the shelf.

"When did you get to be so charming?" Gideon asked.

"You best just shut up unless you are planning on thanking me. I probably saved you from that girl murdering your sorry carcass. You could stand to learn a thing or two from me about charm. I've seen asses with more tact," Jack admonished.

"Where'd you learn a word like chivalry?" Gideon asked mischievously.

"I'm a heap smarter than you give me credit for being. Sometimes I don't know why I bother with you."

Chloe returned with the broom, ending Jack's lecture.

"I've never seen you two before today. Where are you from?" Chloe asked.

"We're from Boulder, in the Colorado Territory, ma'am. We just got into town," Gideon answered.

"Well, you certainly know how to make a grand entrance – I'll give you that. Please call me Chloe."

As they were cleaning up the mess, a middle-aged man entered the store from the back. "What happened here?" he asked in a heavy Irish brogue.

Looking up, Chloe said, "Hi, Pa. Willis Schultz and his men tried to take some supplies when I told him that his credit was cut off. These gentlemen stopped them and things got kind of ugly."

Chloe's pa eyed the men suspiciously. "Nothing like a pretty girl to make a young buck grow bold and assertive," he said.

Gideon and Chloe colored at the remark.

"I'm paying for the damages. I'm sorry to have caused you trouble," Gideon said in hopes of making a better impression.

"I'm Sean McIntire, by the way. Chloe should have introduced us. You're fine by me. I'd rather suffer a loss through an honorable man's actions than be pilfered."

Gideon and Jack introduced themselves and shook the Irishman's hand.

After cleaning up the mess, Gideon paid for the damages and Jack bought some pipe tobacco. Chloe's mood had improved considerably and she gave the men a big smile as they departed.

Out on the boardwalk, Jack said, "I think you're trying to get us killed on our first day in town. For the life of me, I don't know what's gotten into you. You aren't the law here. You need to lighten up – maybe you need to pay a visit to a whore."

"I couldn't just let him leave without paying for his things," Gideon protested.

"That's debatable. That's what the law is for. And besides, you could have tried reasoning with him instead of making it a confrontation. You all but challenged him to a fight."

"I get your point. I'll do better. Let's go find your brother."

"We wasted too much time in the store cleaning up your mess. It's getting late in the day and we need to get a room. We'll find George tomorrow. I'm getting hungry," Jack groused.

After getting a room at the hotel and putting their horses up at the livery stable, Gideon and Jack walked to a café that the hotel clerk had recommended. The place was well-lit and clean looking with checkered tablecloths and a waitress that liked to flirt with all the male customers. Both men had their hearts set on steak. They ordered T-bones with potatoes, and corn, and didn't have to wait long for the food to be delivered.

"That Chloe is quite a little filly," Jack said as he cut his meat.

"I suppose if you like them ungrateful for help," Gideon said before taking a sip of coffee.

Jack let out a chortle. "I know you're not as dense as you sound sometimes. She had a right to be upset. I thought she calmed down right nicely after I captivated her with my mountain man charm. You could learn a lesson or two from old Jack."

Gideon shook his head and smiled. "Yes, you are right. I could have handled things better. It's not like I'm looking for a woman anyway."

The men finished their meals, and were enjoying slices of strawberry pie when Jack spied a lawman entering the café.

"The city marshal just came in and looks like he's headed our way. If he arrests us, just keep your mouth shut. A couple of days in jail will surely be the worst of it. We've made enough enemies for one day," Jack warned.

"May I join you two gentlemen?" the city marshal asked.

"Sure. Help yourself," Jack replied.

"I'm City Marshal Happy Jack Morco." The marshal shook Gideon and Jack's hands before taking a seat beside Jack.

"I'm Farting Jack Dolan. Glad to meet you," the mountain man said, prompting a chuckle from the lawman.

"I'm Gideon Johann."

"I think I got the better of the two nicknames," the city marshal said. "Are you the two boys that have been making such a ruckus around my town?"

Jack straightened his posture and pulled back his head. "I'm afraid that would be us."

Marshal Morco smiled. "I've been hearing about you two all afternoon. What brings you to town?"

Gideon set down his fork. "I came here hoping to hook up with a cattle crew headed back to Texas. I worked as a deputy in Boulder and wanted a change of scenery."

"I rode with Gideon to visit my brother. I'll be heading back to Boulder. Do you know George Dolan?" Jack asked.

The city marshal laughed. "The hatmaker? I'd never guess you'd be brothers. You certainly don't look anything alike."

"That would be him," Jack said.

Looking at Gideon, Marshal Morco said, "Chloe really chewed my ear telling me about you. You made quite a first impression even if it might not have been so good. Sean finally told her that she was going to end up an old spinster if she didn't quit being so hard on all the young men that came into the store."

"I probably could have handled things a little better," Gideon said.

"I doubt it would have turned out any differently. Willis Schultz is a hard one. I've had some run-ins with him myself."

"Are you going to arrest us?" Gideon asked bluntly.

The city marshal laughed again and motioned the waitress to bring him some coffee. "No, I'm not. You came to town a good month before the herds will get here. Most of the riffraff have already arrived though. Why don't you be my deputy until you find a crew you want to work for? I could use the help and you've already been doing my job for me."

The offer took Gideon by surprise. He took a sip of coffee to have some time to mull the offer. Finally, he asked, "Can I think about it overnight?"

"Sure, take your time."

"Thanks for the offer."

"Jack, if you want to stay around for a while, I'd hire you, too. You could spend some time with your brother that way. I have hunch I might need you to keep Gideon from arresting my whole town anyway," Marshal Morco said.

"I'll think that over," Jack said as he looked over at Gideon to see his reaction.

Marshal Morco sat with Gideon and Jack, and talked with them as if he'd known them all his life. He told them all about Ellsworth and asked a lot of questions about Boulder and their pasts. Jack's life as a mountain man particularly interested the lawman. When the marshal finished his coffee, he bid the men adieu.

"That was quite a turn of events," Jack said as he watched the lawman leave the café.

"I didn't want to tell you beforehand, but all the trouble I got into today was for an audition for a job as a deputy," Gideon teased.

"It's a good thing we're amongst other people because all your hot air is making my tummy rumble. And you know what that means," Jack said with a nod of his head and a sly grin.

Chapter 4

The morning after Gideon and Jack arrived in Ellsworth, Gideon woke up feeling as if he were on top of the world. His two skirmishes the previous day, a pretty girl, and a job offer had all played a role in invigorating him. He had gone to sleep as soon as he hit the pillow and slept through the night. Climbing out of bed, he began dressing as if he were a man with somewhere to go and very little time to get there.

Jack, on the other hand, had succumbed to a fitful night of rest. He had listened to Gideon snore in the bed they shared for hours. His original intention to return to Boulder after a short visit with his brother was now clouded by Gideon's recent behavior. The vindictiveness in tracking down of the murderers of the family on the trail and the reckless events of yesterday weighed heavily on Jack's mind. He'd never seen Gideon act so aggressively in his response to tense situations. Jack feared that if he departed before Gideon hooked up with a cattle crew, the young man would end up in trouble whether he worked as a lawman or not. The notion that he cared for Gideon so much, riled him even further. Jack had no children of his own, and couldn't understand how he had come to have paternal feelings for his friend. Such a thing had never happened before now. Also troubling him was the planned meeting with his brother, George. The two men were as different as cats and dogs, and had always had an uneasy relationship.

"I feel like a new man after a sleeping in a real bed again," Gideon said.

With a disgusted look, Jack said, "I wish I could say the same thing. Your snoring kept me up most of the night." He sat up on the edge of the bed and rubbed his face as he tried to banish the lethargic way he felt.

"I've never heard you complain before now, and you've spent plenty of nights beside me on the trail."

"But not in the same bed."

"Get dressed so that we can go have breakfast. You just need a few cups of coffee to get going this morning," Gideon said as he buckled on his gun belt and watched impatiently as Jack slowly stood to retrieve his pants.

By the time Jack had downed his first cup of coffee in the same café where he and Gideon had dined the previous night, he felt as if most of the cobwebs had cleared from his mind. "Have you decided if you'll take the deputy job?" he asked.

"I think that I will. I don't have anything else to do until the herds arrive and I certainly will be running low on money by then. After yesterday's problems, it kind of seems as if I already had the job anyway. What about you?" Gideon replied before picking up a strip of bacon and munching on it.

Jack studied Gideon as his conscience fought over what he should do. "I'm still thinking it over. I'm not sure I can stand being in the same town as George for that long. We're not exactly two peas in a pod."

Gideon raised his eyebrows and nodded his head. "I see. What's the problem? Are you too flatulent for his liking?"

"It's too early in the morning for me to tolerate your attempts at humor. George was always the good boy.

He did well in school and made my parents proud. Me, on the other hand – well, you know me," Jack said wistfully.

"Well, after breakfast, let's go look up George. How long has it been since you've seen him?"

"I guess about five years. He had a shop out East for a long time. I about fell over when he wrote that he lived in Ellsworth. I guess cowboys like new hats after a cattle drive."

"We need to get this reunion a going once we finish breakfast," Gideon said.

After paying for their meals, Gideon and Jack walked around Ellsworth until they saw a shop with 'The Dolan Hat Company' painted on the window. The store was across the street from the jail, and City Marshal Morco sat on a bench in front of his office. He gave the men a wave.

"Looks like this is the place," Gideon said.

"Of course, it's the place. Now get on inside," Jack grumbled.

A small, clean-shaven man sat behind his workbench shaping a hat. "May I help you?" he asked before doing a double take. "Jack, my goodness, what brings you here?"

"Hello, George. This is my friend Gideon Johann. He was coming to Ellsworth so I thought I'd ride with him and say hi," Jack said stiffly.

George walked over to the men and vigorously pumped each man's hand. He seemed genuinely thrilled to see his brother. "This is certainly a surprise. It's so good to see you."

"Likewise. How are you doing?"

"I'm doing fine, and I like Ellsworth. My business and the town are both booming. It gets a little rough around here, but I'm not much for getting out about town, so I do fine," George said. He reached out and patted Jack on the arm before dashing into the back to retrieve a couple of chairs. After putting on a fresh pot of coffee, he sat back down at his bench and talked as he worked.

George proved to be a much more loquacious soul than his brother was. He peppered the two men with questions while adding stories of his time in the cattle town.

Gideon kept looking over at Jack, expecting him to explode at any moment under the constant grilling, but the mountain man seemed thrilled in the interest his brother had taken in him. As for himself, he found the quantity of questions a bit off-putting, but had to concede that George had a knack for making inquiries without seeming as if he were conducting an interrogation. The hatmaker would have been a natural as a lawman.

Once George was satisfied that he was up-to-date on Jack's life, and had gotten to know Gideon, he looked at Jack and asked, "So are you going to take the marshal's offer and be a deputy in our fine town?"

Looking over at Gideon, Jack paused as he gathered his thoughts. He didn't fancy staying in town for a whole month or better, but the unexpected warm reception by George and his concerns for Gideon had overcome his preference for a life of solitude. "I believe I will," he said.

Gideon sat up in his chair and looked over at Jack as if he had pulled a rabbit out of one of George's many hats. "You're going to live in town among all these people until you go back?" he asked skeptically.

"I got plenty of time to get back home before trapping season begins so I don't see why I shouldn't stick around here and spend time with George and keep you from getting killed."

"You're liable to get all citified and start wearing suits and such. Maybe you will find you a woman," Gideon teased.

"Or maybe I'll give you the butt kicking that you could use," Jack warned.

After putting the finishing touches on shaping a hat, George carefully set it down on the workbench. "I have a spare bedroom. You two can stay with me if you can stand sharing the same bed."

Gideon scooted uncomfortably in his chair. "I couldn't take advantage of you like that. Jack can stay with you and I'll stay in the hotel," he said.

"Nonsense, unless Jack wants rid of you. You could share the cost of some groceries and still save your money. I'd enjoy the company," George said.

Jack looked over at Gideon and nodded his head once with authority. "You're staying with us."

"You are the one that complained just this morning about sharing a bed with me," Gideon protested.

"Oh, quit being so sensitive before you turn into a girl. We better get going to tell the marshal that we plan to hire on," Jack said.

"Just as soon as I look at George's hats."

Gideon's Boss of the Plains Stetson had seen better days. He'd purchased it right after the war, and the hat no longer had much shape and the felt had worn slick. Browsing through the various hats, Gideon's eyes fell upon a brown beaver felt one with a pinched front crown crease and three-and-half-inch brim. He tried the hat on and it felt as if it were custom made for his head. Turning to face the mirror on the wall, Gideon admired himself.

Jack shook his head in disgust before bellowing, "Don't be thinking that you're looking dashing and handsome. There's still days I worry that the weight of a hat will collapse that hollow skull of yours."

Reaching into his pocket, Gideon found his money. He paid George for the hat, grinning like a kid in a candy store as he did so. "Let's go before you hurt my feelings," he said before grinning at his reflection one more time.

Outside on the boardwalk, Gideon said, "Seems like you and George get along just fine to me."

Jack took off his hat and scratched his head. "I was as surprised as you were. He no longer seems embarrassed to have me for a brother, and I must admit, I enjoyed his company."

"That's good. I'm glad you're staying around for a while," Gideon said.

The marshal no longer sat outside the jail. They found him inside at his desk. He looked up and grinned when the men entered the building.

"I thought maybe that family reunion was going to take all day. I had to get out of the sun," Marshal Morco said.

"George can be quite the talker," Jack replied.

Marshal Morco nodded his head in agreement. "Well, what's it going to be, boys? Do I have me a couple of new deputies or not?"

"You do," Gideon announced.

"Good. Glad to hear it. I'll have to introduce you to Sheriff Chauncey Whitney and my other deputies."

"When do we start?" Jack asked.

"Today. You can begin this afternoon. I might have neglected to tell you that on most days I'll need you from mid-afternoon until the saloons shut down for the night," the marshal said with an impish grin. "I already know that you boys can handle trouble better than my other deputies, and around here, trouble usually starts when the sun goes down."

"That shouldn't be a problem," Gideon said.

The marshal reached into his middle drawer and pulled out two badges. He hastily swore in his new deputies. "I want you two to stick together as you make your rounds, especially at first. Introduce yourselves wherever you go. The sooner people get to know you, the less likely they'll be to give you trouble," he said.

Jack smiled. "I don't know about that after yesterday. Gideon already made quite a first impression wherever he went."

Gideon looked toward Jack. "You're the one that made the gambler mad. I just kept him from killing you," he protested.

"Burton Rochester is a hothead. Keep your eye on him. He won't forget about getting his comeuppance," the marshal warned.

Sheriff Whitney entered the jail, and the marshal made the introductions before Gideon and Jack took their leave.

"What are we going to do for the rest of the morning?" Jack asked.

"I don't know about you, but I'm headed to the general store to buy some cartridges," Gideon replied with a sly grin.

"Suit yourself, but I have my doubts that a new hat and badge are going to make Chloe find you any more attractive. That train has done left the station," Jack said, bobbling his head with pride at his retort.

Leaving Jack on his own, Gideon crossed the street toward the general store. The mountain man watched him go, and wondered how long his friend's sunny disposition would last. He'd seen Gideon struggle too often in the last couple of months to believe the change of scenery would make a long-lasting change in his friend's happiness. The young man had demons that haunted him, and Jack figured they were still close at hand.

Gideon entered the store to find Chloe behind the counter in an otherwise empty shop.

"Good morning. I need a couple of boxes of Henry .44 caliber rimfire cartridges," Gideon said.

"Are you sure you don't want to break a few things first?" Chloe asked before failing to suppress the smallest of grins.

"No, I couldn't afford many more days like yesterday."

Chloe caught sight of the badge on his shirt. She pulled her head back and pursed her lips. "Don't tell me you're the law now. How did that happen?"

"The marshal seemed a lot more impressed with me preventing you from being robbed than you were. He offered jobs to Jack and me. I worked as a deputy in Boulder," Gideon said in hopes of convincing her that he was qualified for the job.

After retrieving the cartridges from a shelf, Chloe placed them on the counter. "Was the sheriff your uncle or something?" she asked in her attempt to further needle Gideon.

"No, he wasn't. You know, I did apologize yesterday and I'll apologize again today if necessary. I really was trying to help you."

"Yes, you did. I should be more appreciative. Apology accepted. I like your new hat."

Gideon stood up straighter and adjusted the hat. "Thank you. George, the hatmaker, is Jack's brother. Jack rode here with me for a visit. I saw this thing and had to have it," he said proudly.

"I see. It becomes you. That will be one dollar for the cartridges."

He fetched the money from his pocket. "Would you like to go to dinner with me sometime? Taking every meal with Jack can grow a bit tiresome."

Chloe gave a restrained smile. "I don't think that would be a good idea. Nothing personal, but I don't see where we'd have much to talk about, but thank you for the invitation."

Gideon smiled back. "Suit yourself. I'll be seeing you around town." He gave a wink before walking out of the store with his purchase.

Chapter 5

Gideon and Jack spent most of their first day on the job going around town making introductions to all of the Ellsworth storekeepers, saloon owners, and brothel operators. For the most part, they were received warmly, and offered everything from free drinks to a romp with a whore by proprietors looking to ingratiate themselves with the new law officers. Gideon and Jack did partake of a couple of beers, but declined any of the more risqué enticements. They made it through the evening without encountering any troubles, and retired to George's house a little after midnight.

After a few days, the new routine of having their mornings and the first part of the afternoons free, led to boredom. Gideon and Jack had been early risers all their life and didn't know what to do with all the idle time. Jack began relearning the family business from George just to have something to do. Gideon took up reading. He had once had a love for Shakespeare, and now passed his time sitting in the shop trying to reacquaint himself with the writings of the bard as the Dolan brothers made hats.

At three o'clock, the men would stroll out of George's business and start making the rounds. The first few days on the job had been uneventful. They'd broken up a couple of saloon fights and arrested one man for trying to sneak off without paying a whore that had been foolish enough to allow sampling of the goods before the money had changed hands. As they were walking down the main street, a man ran out of the Red Rose Saloon waving his arms for them.

"Come quick. He's going to kill Teddy," the man yelled before running back inside of the business.

Gideon and Jack took off in a jog to the saloon. The crowd inside was up on their feet, some of them standing on chairs, as they watched Sean McIntire unmercifully beat Teddy Calhoun with an ax handle.

"I ought to kill you," Sean yelled with every few swings of the stick.

Teddy was crouched down doing his best to protect his head as Sean rained down wild blows that landed all over the body. Gideon tackled Sean, knocking the storekeeper to the floor. He tried to use his weight to hold him down, but in the Irishman's irate state, he managed to get on all fours. Jack added his considerable heft onto the men. The extra weight took Sean back down, and flattened Gideon in the process, smashing him to the point that breathing was difficult. From atop the pile, Jack reached over and removed the ax handle from Sean's grasp.

After taking a deep breath to refill his lungs, Gideon paused a long moment before saying, "Sean, we're going to let you up, but if you don't behave, I'll take my revolver and lay you out. Do you understand me?"

"Yes. Please get off me. I can't get any air," Sean pleaded.

Jack got to his feet, allowing Gideon and Sean to do the same. Teddy remained squatted over with his arms over his head as if unconvinced the violence had come to an end.

"Get to your feet," Jack ordered Teddy.

Teddy used the bar to pull himself to a standing position, and kept a hand on it to steady himself. He had a nasty looking knot in the middle of his forehead and the left side of his jaw was beginning to swell. Sean had worked him over thoroughly.

"What's this all about?" Gideon asked.

Using his hand to comb his hair back in place, Sean said, "Teddy needed a good beating."

"And why is that?"

"I have nothing further to say on the matter," Sean said.

Turning to Teddy, Gideon asked, "And what do you have to say?"

"Not a thing, deputy. Not a thing."

"Have you two ever had problems before today?" Jack asked.

"No, sir."

Gideon eyed the two men, trying to guess what had happened between them and why neither would talk. "Sean, I'm sorry, but we have to take you to jail." He took Sean by the arm.

Teddy held up his hand. "Stop. I'll not press charges. Sean and I have been in this town since the beginning. There's no cause to sully each other's name. Excuse me, but I need to sit down." He sat down in a chair at the nearest table and pulled his pocket watch from his vest to see if it had survived the beating.

Jack glanced over at Gideon and got a shrug for a response.

Releasing Sean's arm, Gideon said, "Jack, why don't you stay here and see to Teddy. I'm going to walk Sean back to the store."

"Sounds about right to me," Jack responded.

Sean headed for the door with Gideon following close behind him. The storekeeper walked briskly, not saying a word. He entered the store and headed for his office in the back.

Chloe stood on a stool, dusting a shelf. She furrowed her forehead in confusion at seeing her father come through the front door. "Pa, I thought you were still in the back."

Gideon tipped his hat as he walked past her. Sean tried to slam the door to the office, but Gideon blocked the entrance with his foot. The Irishman took a seat at his desk and pulled a bottle of whiskey from a drawer. He grabbed two glasses and poured a generous amount into each.

"If you aren't going to leave, you might as well have a drink with me," Sean said.

After closing the door behind him, Gideon took a seat across from Sean. He picked up the glass and took a sip of the whiskey. "Smooth. That's some fine liquor."

"Irish whiskey. When you like liquor as well as my countrymen do, they make a point of knowing how to make the stuff the right way," Sean said, smiling for the first time.

"Are you going to tell me what just happened?"

"No, the matter is settled. I'll say nothing more about it."

"You don't strike me as the type of man that takes an ax handle to another man for no good reason. Something sure riled you," Gideon said.

"Damn it, man, mind your own business and drink your whiskey. The troubles are now over with," Sean yelled. In his agitated state, his Irish brogue sounded so thick that he was hard to understand.

"It won't be settled if one of you tries to kill the other one. It's my job to see that doesn't happen," Gideon said, his voice rising.

"If I planned on killing Teddy Calhoun, he'd already be dead. You have nothing to worry about now. Teddy won't bother me either," Sean bellowed.

Chloe had been listening outside the door. She opened it and stormed into the office. "For God's sake, I'll tell him if you won't. Teddy came into the store when I was here alone. He got grabby with me, and when I tried to push him away, he tore the front of my dress. I kneed him good. That took all his amorous ideas right out of him. Before I could get home to change clothes, Pa came in and saw my dress. Otherwise, he'd be none the wiser. I knew he'd do something stupid."

"Sean, you should have come to the jail and reported what happened instead of doing this," Gideon admonished.

"The only thing that would have accomplished is to give my daughter a reputation as a loose woman. You know how stories get changed all around, and I'll not have her good name soiled over the likes of Teddy Calhoun," Sean said, popping his desk with his hand.

Gideon leaned back in his chair, exhaled loudly, and rubbed his scar. "You sure made a spectacle of things for somebody not wanting to draw attention to the situation, but I suppose Teddy won't be bragging about any of this either."

"Not if he knows what's good for him," Sean said.

"I thought you said this is over with."

"It is as long as he keeps his big mouth shut."

After taking off his hat, Gideon ran his hand through his mane of hair. "I'll talk to Teddy. Do I have your word that you'll leave him alone?"

"On my honor."

Gideon drained the whiskey from his glass. "I better get back over to the saloon. Jack will be wondering what happened to me." He stood and walked toward the front of the store.

Chloe shut the door to the office and followed Gideon.

"Thank you for your help," she said.

Stopping and turning, Gideon said, "I'm just doing my job."

"Maybe, but you could have sure gone about things a lot differently. Marshal Morco would have."

"Really? The marshal seems like a pretty good guy to me."

"Oh, he is as long as he doesn't get angered. The Happy Jack can disappear in a heartbeat. He would have beaten the ax handle out of Pa's hand. He likes to fight," Chloe warned.

"I'll keep that in mind. I'll also remember to ask permission before I ever get grabby with you," Gideon said with a wink, hoping to lighten the mood.

"Goodbye, Gideon."

"You take care."

Gideon walked back to the saloon and found Teddy still sitting in a chair. The knots on his head and jaw had swollen further, putting the saloonkeeper in much pain. Jack sat at the table with him, drinking a beer to pass the time.

"Is there a place we can talk in private?" Gideon asked.

"Sure.   Follow me," Teddy said before standing gingerly. He slowly led the men to a back room.

"Sean gave me his word that this is over. Will you do the same?"

"I didn't start it and I have no reason to continue it. You have my word."

"Oh, I think you did start it. I know what prompted this whole thing. Sean is more worried about Chloe's reputation than anything. I don't know why you'd brag about what you did, but if you ever do, I'll cut you like a steer. You won't ever think about looking at a woman again. Do I make myself clear?" Gideon asked.

"I understand. I made an error in judgement," Teddy mumbled as he rubbed his jaw.

"That you did. You're going to be mighty sore after the way Sean worked you over. We're leaving now. Stay out of trouble," Gideon warned.

Outside the saloon, Gideon filled Jack in on all the details of what had caused Sean's behavior.

"Do you think this is the end of it?" Jack asked.

"Oh, yeah. Sean's a good man that was just defending his daughter's honor. Teddy might not be the most upstanding citizen in Ellsworth, but he's smart enough to let this blow over."

"I have a feeling this is the beginning of a challenging evening," Jack said as he scanned the street.

Chapter 6

"I think all the saloons must have been serving mean beer last night," Jack said as he sat at the table waiting for George to finish cooking eggs and bacon for breakfast.

"Well, I hope they don't serve any of it tonight. I don't think I could take two nights in a row of all the shenanigans we dealt with," Gideon replied as he touched his cheek.

The two men had broken up three saloon fights and arrested a man that had fired his gun at another card player after losing all his money at poker. Luckily, the shot hadn't hit anyone. Gideon had been on the receiving end of a blow to the cheek when he'd stepped between two of the brawlers. He had a bruise on his cheek to show for his efforts.

"I'll stick to making hats. They don't hit . . ." George said.

A knock on the door interrupted him in mid-sentence. He scurried to the front of the house. A moment later, he returned to the kitchen with Deputy Webb Schafer accompanying him.

"The marshal wants you both down at the Red Rose right now," Webb said.

Hearing mention of the Red Rose caused Gideon to look up at Deputy Schafer with trepidation. "What's the problem?" he asked reluctantly.

"Somebody killed Teddy Calhoun while he slept."

The news caused Gideon's shoulders to shudder and he could feel the hairs standing on his neck. He and Jack glanced at each other. The exchange conferred as much as if they'd had a whole conversation on the subject. Neither man could imagine Sean McIntire being so foolish as to murder Teddy the night after giving him a sound beating.

"Does the marshal know who did it?" Jack asked.

"He knows about what Sean McIntire did yesterday and how you didn't arrest him. He's not happy," Webb said.

Without wasting any more time, Gideon and Jack grabbed their hats and buckled on their gun belts. They walked with the deputy to the saloon and entered through the front door. An old woman that neither Gideon nor Jack had ever seen before, sat at a table crying. Deputy Schafer led them upstairs into the first room off the landing.

Teddy Calhoun lay in his bed as if he were still sleeping except that his throat had been slashed from ear to ear. He'd also been stabbed in the heart through the bedcovers. The bed was drenched in blood. So much so that it was hard to imagine that Teddy still had any left in his arteries.

"Quite a mess, isn't it? Somebody seemed to be pretty handy with a knife," Marshal Morco said.

"That it is," Jack said.

In a tone short on patience, the marshal asked, "Why didn't you arrest Sean yesterday?"

"We were going to, but Teddy refused to press charges," Gideon answered.

"Looks like you should have done it anyway."

"I don't think Sean did this. I had both men's word that this was settled," Gideon stated.

"Well, it seems mighty coincidental to me that Teddy is dead now. Don't you agree? I heard about the fight yesterday and wondered why you didn't bring Sean in. It was the talk of the town. It's not often that two of our more prosperous citizens square off against each other. Folks said Sean kept yelling how he ought to kill Teddy as he wacked him. What brought all this about?"

Gideon looked at Jack. He hated betraying confidences, but knew there was no way he could refuse to tell the marshal what he knew. "Teddy was in the general store alone with Chloe. He grabbed her and tore her dress. Sean wanted to make sure it never happened again."

"That sounds about like Teddy. He had a weakness for pretty ladies."

"Who found Teddy?" Jack asked.

"The old lady he pays to clean this place and fix his meals. She brought him his breakfast this morning and found him. She's quite beside herself."

"Was there anybody else in the saloon?"

"Just Teddy's two whores. I like to have never gotten them woke up to ask them if they heard anything. I think they had too many free drinks last night. They never heard a thing and I don't think they did it. Both of them were beside themselves worrying about where they were going to go."

"Did Teddy have any enemies?" Gideon asked.

The marshal chuckled. "Oh, at least a couple. Lonnie Wilson over at the Cowboy Palace used to be Teddy's partner in this place until Teddy found out Lonnie had been cheating him. They got into quite the brawl over that. And everybody in town except for Kenneth Shepherd knows that Teddy is banging Kenneth's wife while he works all day as our telegraph operator. I'm sure there are others, too. Just can't think of anyone else off the top of my head."

"Sounds like we have some suspects then," Gideon said.

"Maybe, but I want you to go arrest Sean for murder. Look for the knife and bloody clothes at his house and in the store while you are at it."

"What? We can't arrest Sean. We have no evidence that he did this," Gideon protested.

"We have circumstantial evidence and we may find some real evidence. That's enough for now."

"No grand jury would bring this to trial."

"I've seen men hang on less. Men that I had a pretty good hunch were probably innocent. Our job is to arrest them, and the grand jury and a jury of Sean's peers can decide if he is innocent. Now go do what I said."

"Couldn't the grand jury be convened before we arrest Sean? Let them decide if we need to arrest him," Gideon said.

"Just go do it," the marshal yelled.

Gideon pulled off his hat and stood defiantly. "No, I'll quit before I arrest an innocent man. I've been a deputy in two other towns and I've never seen a man arrested without cause."

Marshal Morco smiled. "I like you. You got grit – I'll give you that, son. I'll tell you what I'll do – you and Jack can have the rest of the day to find a reason for me to think somebody other than Sean did this, but if you have nothing, you arrest Sean. You need to quit assuming Sean is innocent. I'm sure you've known men that you've trusted and they deceived you. I like Sean, and I hope he is innocent. If you still think he's not guilty afterward, you can spend all the time you need trying to find the real murderer. I wouldn't take any pleasure in hanging an innocent man."

Rubbing his scar, Gideon's mind raced on what to do. The marshal had planted a seed of doubt about Sean's innocence even if the deputy's gut told him otherwise. Gideon quickly came to the conclusion that the only chance he had to give Sean a fair shake was to stay on the job. "I can live with that."

"Very well. I like a good compromise," the marshal said.

Gideon noticed Teddy's clothes draped over a chair in a corner of the room. The saloonkeeper's wallet lay on the floor near there. Gideon walked over and picked it up. The wallet was empty of any money. "Looks like our killer also did some robbing. If this was a revenge killing, I wouldn't think Sean would be also robbing the man," he said as he rifled through the clothes. "Didn't Teddy wear a pocket watch?"

"The robbery might be just a ruse, and I have no idea if Teddy wore a watch. Most times, I just watched his hands pour me a beer. I'm going to miss old Teddy. He ran a pretty fair saloon," Marshal Morco said wistfully.

"I'm going to talk to the old lady. There's nothing much else to glean from in here," Gideon said before walking out of the room with Jack following behind him.

The old woman still sat at the table. She'd quit crying, but seemed to be at a loss with what to do with herself. In her hands she held a hankie that she worked tirelessly between her fingers.

"Ma'am, I'm Deputy Johann and this is Deputy Dolan. What's your name?"

"Mrs. Mooney."

"Mrs. Mooney, did you notice anything unusual before you found Teddy this morning?" Gideon asked.

"I always come into the saloon from the alley entrance. I have my own key, but it wasn't locked this morning. I thought it odd, but I figured Teddy forgot to lock it last night. It wouldn't be the first time."

"Anything else?"

"No, not that I can think of. I don't know what I'm going to do. I depended on the money that Teddy paid me," Mrs. Mooney said.

At a loss on how to respond to the woman, Gideon fumbled out, "Maybe one of the other saloons will hire you." He reached into his pocket and pulled out a five-dollar piece. "I hope this might hold you over until you find something."

Gideon and Jack walked to the back of the saloon to examine the rear entrance. The door showed no signs of forced entry.

"Somebody either had a key or Teddy picked a bad night to forget to lock the dang thing," Jack said.

"I wonder if Lonnie Wilson still has keys to this place. I wasn't too impressed with him when we introduced ourselves the other day," Gideon said.

"Worth looking into."

Letting out a sigh, Gideon said, "Let's go talk to Sean and get that over with."

The men walked down the alley and over to the general store. Sean and Chloe were busy restocking shelves when they entered the building.

"Top of the morning to you. What can we do for you gentlemen?" Sean greeted.

Chloe sensed that something was wrong from the men's expressions. She turned and faced the deputies. "What is it?"

"Teddy Calhoun was murdered in his sleep," Gideon said.

The color drained from Sean's face. "You can't think that I'd be addled-brained enough to kill Sean after giving him a whipping, do you?"

"No, I don't, but I have to ask you some questions all the same. Where were you last night?" Gideon asked.

"Chloe and I spent the evening in our home. I retired to my room around ten o'clock."

"We never left the house," Chloe added.

"Would your wife vouch for you, too?"

"Margaret has been dead going on five years."

"Oh, I didn't know. I'm sorry for your loss. Sean, do I have your word that you didn't kill Teddy?" Gideon asked.

"On my daughter's life I swear I didn't murder Teddy."

"The marshal has ordered me to arrest you at the end of the day if we don't find evidence to point to somebody else. I'm sorry, but I wanted to give you time to prepare yourself."

Chloe threw her hands up in the air. "You can't arrest Pa without any evidence. Marshal Morco just wants the case closed. What kind of man are you that you would go along with such a travesty?"

Gideon stood there, not knowing what to say.

Jack took off his hat and stepped forward. "Ma'am, Gideon did threaten to quit, but we quickly came to realize that the best way to clear your pa's name is to stay on the job. The marshal assured us that we could continue to investigate this even if we have to arrest Sean later today. Marshal Morco doesn't want to convict an innocent man. I promise you that we will do our best to get to the bottom of this."

Placing her hands on her hips, Chloe said, "My apologies. Thank you for that reassurance. I can't bear the thought of Pa being in jail."

Rubbing the back of his neck, Gideon said, "There's a good chance that is going to happen. It will be pure luck to solve this in a day. The marshal wanted me to look around the store and your home. Do I have your permission?"

"Help yourself. I have nothing to hide," Sean said.

Gideon and Jack searched the store and after finding nothing incriminating, Sean walked them to his home. Once again, they worked their way through a clean, well-kept house, and as expected, found nothing to suggest that Sean McIntire had committed the murder. After accompanying Sean back to the store, Gideon thanked the storekeeper before departing.

"What now?" Jack asked.

"Let's go talk to Lonnie," Gideon replied.

The Cowboy Palace Saloon had not yet opened for business, and the door remained locked. Gideon pounded on it three separate times before one of the saloon's whores came and opened it. She was dressed in a sheer housecoat that left no doubt that she wasn't wearing anything underneath of it.

Upon seeing the law officers, the whore turned her head and yelled, "Hey, Rosie, that new deputy you've been hankering for with the pretty blue eyes is here."

"Ma'am, is Lonnie in?" Gideon asked.

"He's probably in something about now. Come in. I'm Trella, by the way."

Rosie emerged from a back room wearing only a chemise tucked into her drawers. Her wild, flaming red hair framed a pleasing face that smiled suggestively at Gideon. "Hi," she said.

Gideon tipped his hat as he and Jack followed Trella up the stairs to the second floor.

"He's in there," Trella said, pointing toward a room.

Beating loudly on the door, Gideon yelled, "This is Deputy Johann. Open up. We need to talk."

"Go away. You can come back later," a voice replied.

"No, you need to open the door."

"Go to hell."

Testing the doorknob, Gideon found it unlocked. He drew his Remington revolver and entered the room. Lonnie's eyes lost their droopy appearance at seeing the gun shoved in his face. A woman lying beside him, slept on through the commotion.

"I don't appreciate your tone. I suggest you change it now," Gideon said.

"Fine. Put that damn gun away. Now what do you want?" Lonnie asked.

"Somebody murdered Teddy Calhoun last night. Where were you?"

The news seemed to catch Lonnie off guard. His mouth tightened and his eyes wrinkled in apparent sadness at learning the news. He ran his hand through his hair before rubbing his mouth. "Teddy is dead? That's a hard thing to imagine. We weren't friends anymore, but all the troubles between us happened a long time ago. I worked the bar all evening and then came up here with Delaware."

"Do you still have keys to the Red Rose?"

"I might have an old set around here somewhere, but Teddy changed all the locks after we parted ways. You can ask Mrs. Mooney. He would have had to give her a new one," Lonnie said.

Gideon glanced over at Delaware. She remained oblivious to the world. "What's wrong with her?" he asked.

"She's an addict."

"See if she'll wake up."

Lonnie began vigorously shaking Delaware and calling her name. The whore moaned a couple of times before waking in a panic. With a flurry of fists and fingernails, she attacked Lonnie, forcing him to shove her away and nearly sending her off the bed.

"Damn it, Delaware. It's just me," Lonnie yelled as he rubbed a claw mark on his arm.

The woman came to her senses and noticed the two lawmen standing by the bed. "What do they want?"

"Did you spend all night with Lonnie?" Gideon asked.

"Yeah, as far as I can remember," she replied.

Gideon sighed and shook his head. "We're done here for now. Let's go."

Trella and Rosie were sitting at a table drinking coffee as Gideon and Jack descended the stairs.

"Hey, deputy, come visit me sometime. I'll show those big blue eyes something they ain't ever seen before," Rosie called out before blowing a kiss.

Gideon made a quick exit of the saloon before the whores had a chance to see him blush.

"You're as red as a beet," Jack said with a chuckle while slapping his legs.

"Just hush. We need to concentrate on the job at hand. Unless Lonnie is the greatest actor since John Wilkes Booth, I don't think he's our killer. Delaware's alibi for him is all but useless, but he seemed genuinely upset over Teddy's death."

"I don't know about Lonnie. I'm still not convinced it isn't him. I'm sure he heard about the fight, and he strikes me as smart enough to take advantage of it. That might have been all an act up there for all you know, and he'll talk that whore into whatever he wants her to believe. She'd be lucky to remember her name," Jack said.

"I think you're wrong, but we do need to keep on open mind."

"I guess we need to head to the telegraph office. It's probably not safe for you to loiter outside this saloon anyway with that redhead just beyond the door," Jack said, still grinning at Gideon's embarrassment.

When Gideon and Jack entered the telegraph office, they found Kenneth Shepherd sitting at his desk scribbling frantically while the telegraph machine chattered away. The telegraph operator was a little man with a pencil-thin mustache and spectacles. Once the machine grew silent, Kenneth finished his scrawling before pulling off his glasses. He looked up to see who had entered the office.

"May I help you gentlemen?"

Gideon pulled off his hat and held it in both hands as he contemplated what to say. "Mr. Shepherd, I don't know if word has spread yet, but Teddy Calhoun was murdered in his sleep," he said before pausing to try to choose his next words.

"Yes, the news is all over town by now. I suppose you are here because Gloria was sleeping with Teddy, and you wonder if I killed him out of jealousy," Kenneth said in a brazen tone.

"Yes, sir. That about sums it up."

"I know this whole town thinks I'm an oblivious fool, but I've known about them since nearly the beginning of their tryst. My wife and I have an understanding. I get what I need from our arrangement and she gets what she needs. Ours might not be the most moral of unions, but it certainly is pragmatic. And yes, I knew about Sean beating Teddy, but I didn't use that as a cover to kill him. I spent the night with Gloria – you can ask her. Gloria didn't do it either. I'm a light sleeper, and she wakes me up every time she rolls over. I would have known if she had left the house during the night," Kenneth said.

"I guess that about covers everything. Do you have any ideas on who might have killed him?" Gideon asked.

"Not anybody that wouldn't have done it a long time ago if they were so inclined. I surely do not believe that Sean McIntire is capable of murder. You have your hands full on this one."

"Thank you for your cooperation, Mr. Shepherd," Gideon said before leaving.

Outside, Jack said, "That was the likes of nothing I've ever seen before now. That little man is a strange fellow."

"You can say that again. Let's go talk to his wife and then get something to eat. I'm about starved. That bacon smelled so good this morning. George probably ate all of it," Gideon said.

Gloria Shepherd was an attractive woman with fine features and an air of refinement. Her regal bearing did not lend itself to the notion that Kenneth or Teddy would be suitable partners of her choosing. Word had not yet reached her about Teddy's death, and when Gideon told her, she broke down in uncontrollable sobs and hurled herself onto a couch. Minutes passed before she regained her composure. The interview that followed proved as fruitless as all the others had.

Gideon and Jack walked to the diner feeling dejected that they were no closer to solving the crime than when they started out that morning. After eating, they spent the rest of the day talking to townsfolk in hopes of finding someone that had seen something unusual or could provide any additional suspects. They also found out where Mrs. Mooney lived and paid her a visit. She confirmed that Teddy had new locks installed after he and Lonnie parted ways. As the time neared five o'clock, they drudged to McIntire's General Store.

"Sean, we didn't learn anything today," Gideon said when they entered the store.

The Irishman looked defeated. His face had a sallow appearance and his posture sagged. He held his mouth so tightly closed that his lips all but disappeared. Chloe broke down in tears and had to be comforted by her father. He took her in his arms and patted his daughter's back.

"This can't be happening," she wailed into her pa's shoulder.

"Keep your faith. That's what we have to do," Sean assured her.

Feeling as if he could crawl under a rock, Gideon looked up at the ceiling as he searched his mind for some words of comfort. Jack stood beside him shifting his weight from one foot to the other and rubbing his hands together in agitation.

"I promise I won't stop trying to find out who killed Teddy," Gideon said. He thought his words sounded as hollow as a rotted out tree, and he had a hard time making eye contact with Sean.

"I know you will. I can tell that you're a fine man with backbone," Sean said. "Please keep an eye out for Chloe. We have friends that will help her, but they don't wear a badge."

"You have my word."

Sean gave his daughter a kiss on the cheek before stepping away. "Let's go make the marshal happy."

Chapter 7

When the clock struck six o'clock in the afternoon, Chloe pulled the shades down in the store, and with hands trembling from nervous exhaustion, locked the door. As she walked home alone, she felt as if she were on a march to the gallows. Her heart raced and she felt flushed as she tried to get a handle on all that had happened that day. She felt racked with guilt for not concealing the torn dress from her pa, and blamed herself for all that had transpired since then. Her father would have never beaten Teddy if she had succeeded with her plan, and even if Teddy had been murdered anyway, nobody would have ever considered her pa as a suspect.

"Where is your pa, dear?" Mrs. Greely asked. She lived across the street from Chloe and her pa, and was standing out in her yard retrieving laundry off the clothesline. The middle-aged woman had tried to serve as a surrogate mother since the death of Chloe's momma even as she raised her own bunch of children.

"Oh, Mrs. Greely, it's terrible," Chloe said. She began sniffling in an attempt to hold back the tears, but lost the fight. Her shoulders trembled and a little yelp escaped her lips.

Mrs. Greely engulfed Chloe into her bosom, patting the young woman's back as the sobbing started.

"What is it?" Mrs. Greely asked as she released Chloe after the weeping had subsided.

Chloe explained all that had happened since yesterday morning.

"Marshal Morco is more interested in protecting his badge than he is Ellsworth's good citizens. I've never heard of such a thing," Mrs. Greely said.

"The whole thing seems like one of those bad dreams where you can't make yourself wake up. I still have a hard time wrapping my head around the notion that the marshal felt he could make an arrest without any evidence pointing to my pa. I don't know if Pa will survive in jail."

"Your father has as much character and strength as any man I've ever known. He'll be fine. And I bet he'll be out soon. They can't convict him without some proof that he did it."

"The last few years have been hard on Pa since Momma died. I don't know if he has the wherewithal to withstand another torment."

"Mr. Bryant is the finest lawyer in town. Did you go talk to him?" Mrs. Greely asked.

The question caused Chloe to close her eyes and cover her mouth in consternation. "Pa and I never even talked about a lawyer. This whole thing has made me so addle-brained that I never even thought about it."

"You can do that first thing in the morning. Mr. Bryant will help you."

"Thank you, Mrs. Greely. I do feel better."

"Why don't you have supper with us?"

"I appreciate the offer, but I think I want to be alone. I wouldn't be much company right now, and I don't want to cry in front of your children," Chloe said.

"Well, if you need me, you know where I live. Just come on over," Mrs. Greely said.

As Chloe entered her home, she wondered why her family had ever moved to the rowdy town of Ellsworth.

They had gotten by just fine with the store they ran back in Fort Leavenworth, where she had been born. After they moved to Ellsworth, the family had prospered, but at a cost. They had suffered through their fair share of encounters with the town's rough inhabitants, and her mother had died of the influenza that had plagued the town one winter. With her death, Chloe had lost her best friend and confidante. She didn't have many friends, and the ones she had, were much older than she was. There weren't many women her own age in the cow town except for a few that were already married and busy raising babies, and the sporting girls. She knew the old ladies already considered her a spinster at the ripe old age of twenty-four. And truth be told, maybe she already was one. She had had numerous suitors, but not many that she considered marriage material. Most of them had been either wild cowboys or men that lived on the shady side of the law. She had come to accept the idea that marriage was more than likely not in the cards for her.

Chloe started fixing supper to get her mind off everything. She had the food ready to eat before realizing she had fixed a meal for two people. The mistake stole the last bit of strength she had left. With the realization that she would be spending the first night of her life alone, she dropped into a chair, burying her head in her arms. The crying broke loose again like a dam giving way in a flood, and didn't stop until she made herself sick.

∞

"I would have headed back to Boulder if I'd known I'd have to work this hard," Jack said as he and Gideon walked toward George's home.

"I might have gone with you," Gideon joked.

The time was well past midnight, and the two men had been on the job since Deputy Schafer had fetched them that morning after Teddy Calhoun's body had been found. They had spent the evening patrolling the saloons. The one saving grace of the day was that the night had gone without any trouble.

"I'm headed straight to bed," Jack said after they had entered the house.

"I'm sure I'll be joining you shortly," Gideon said as he headed to the kitchen and lit an oil lamp.

Gideon reached for his whiskey bottle he had stored on a shelf in the room. Though his body ached for the bed, his mind raced like a train on a straight downhill run. He poured himself a glass of whiskey and sat down at the table. After taking his first sip, Gideon held the glass up to the light and studied the amber colored alcohol. The sound of a creaking floorboard broke him out of his reverie.

Jack ambled into the kitchen as if it took all his strength to put one foot in front of the other. He dropped into the chair across from Gideon with enough force to make a popping sound.

"So what's bothering you?" Jack asked.

Gideon grinned at the old mountain man, realizing how well Jack really knew him. Sometimes he sold Jack short, but truth be told, there wasn't much that got past the old codger.

"Everything, I guess. I'm worried about Sean and Chloe. The marshal isn't being fair about this, and I would think he'd worry about looking bad if we find the real murderer," Gideon said.

"He's not concerned about that because he doesn't think we'll find anybody else. We have our work cut out for us on this one. Sean ain't convicted yet. I suspect he's liked well enough that his neighbors will give him the benefit of the doubt if things were to go that far," Jack said.

"I hope you're right," Gideon said. He took another sip of whiskey and resumed staring at the liquid.

"What else is eating at you?"

Gideon made a little snicker sound. Something about the day had made him nostalgic for his little hometown and all he had left behind there. He knew he'd never mentioned a thing to Jack about the place, but asked, "Have I ever told you about Last Stand?"

"I just remember on the day that Sheriff Howell hired you that you said you were from there – that's all."

"Last Stand was fine little place to live. I grew up on a little ranch outside of town with good parents. The only girl I ever loved came from there. Her name was Abby Schone. She was as sweet as they come and a pretty thing. And my friend Ethan Oakes was like the brother I never had. After my momma died, my pa and I got this foolish notion to join the war. I saw a lot of terrible things in that damn war, and Pa got killed. I wrote Abby and Ethan all the time. In fact, I got teased about it while sitting around the campfire writing the letters. Until one day I just stopped. Never wrote them again or ever went back to Last Stand. They probably all think I'm dead, I guess. I would imagine they're both married by now," Gideon said. He couldn't stand to look

Jack in the eye as he talked so he continued to stare at his whiskey.

"Maybe you should write them now or go pay a visit to Last Stand. Might do all of you some good."

"And what would I say?"

"You tell me."

"I guess I'd say that I wasn't worthy of their love and friendship, and that I had an evilness that they didn't know about – heck, that I didn't even know about. Wouldn't that be quite a letter?" Gideon said as he finally looked at Jack.

"Damn, Gideon. I wish you would tell me what you did that haunts you so. Confession is good for the soul. Whatever it is, I can tell you that you're not evil. An evil man does not destroy his life by being consumed with guilt – he just justifies his actions and goes on doing the same thing over and over."

"I'll take what I did to my grave. I couldn't bear for my own ears to hear those words," Gideon said.

The light reflected the tears welling up in Gideon's eyes. They made Jack feel like crying, too. He wished that one of the many Indian medicines he knew how to make would fix a man with a broken spirit.

"Son, I wish I knew how to fix you, cause I'd give just about anything to do it," Jack said.

Gideon smiled. "You're a good friend, Jack. I wish you could, too. Let's go to bed." He tipped up his glass and finished off the drink.

The vision of the little boy came to Gideon as soon as he closed his eyes, but exhaustion won out over the apparition, and the deputy drifted off into sound sleep.

Chapter 8

A good night of sleep had put Gideon in a much better frame of mind. He chowed down on his eggs and bacon with a renewed determination to solve Teddy Calhoun's murder. While he devoured the breakfast, Jack and George exchanged glances as they watched him eat.

"What's put the giddy-up into you?" Jack asked.

"I don't know – just feeling better. Would you rather have me all hangdog?" Gideon asked.

"Not by any means. You are one complicated man, Gideon Johann, – I'll give you that."

With a big grin, Gideon shrugged his shoulders as he tore off a chunk of bacon with his teeth.

After walking with the Dolan brothers to the business section of town, Gideon headed for the livery stable. His horse hadn't been ridden in days, and he wanted to exercise the gelding. Gideon liked to use his time riding for contemplation, and figured he would plot his next move in solving Teddy's murder while on horseback.

A lanky boy of about sixteen with blond hair and a big, toothy smile emerged from the barn. "Can I help you?" he asked.

"Good morning. I've just started boarding my horse here, but I've never seen you before today. Are you new?" Gideon asked.

"I've been here about a month. Mr. Nance usually keeps me busy cleaning out the stalls and doing other jobs related to the wrong end of a horse. I'm Martin

Sanders," the boy said, offering his hand and flashing his big grin again.

Gideon shook Martin's hand while studying the young man. He could have sworn he'd met him somewhere before today, but couldn't recall the place. "I'm Gideon Johann – one of the new deputies in town. Have you ever been to Boulder or Cheyenne? I could swear we've met somewhere before today."

"I've never been west of Ellsworth. I'm from a town that's now called Junction City."

"You sure look familiar. Maybe you just remind me of somebody I once knew. I've come to take Rowdy for a ride. He's the roan that will take a plug out of you if you're not careful."

"I know the horse you're talking about, and I've got the bite mark to prove it. I'll be right back with him," Martin said before disappearing into the barn.

Gideon chose to take the road north out of town for his ride. Because he and Jack had arrived in Ellsworth coming from the west, he figured he'd check out some new territory in a different direction. As he rode, he racked his brain trying to place Martin. The young man's appearance sure triggered a sense of having met before, but for the life of him, he could not place Martin. Giving up on the endeavor, Gideon put Rowdy into a lope, and locked his body into the rhythm of the horse's movement. The pace felt exhilarating, and gave him a sense of freedom he seldom felt. He let Rowdy run until the horse had worked up a lather before reining him down to a walk. Up ahead, he saw three riders approaching. As they drew near, Gideon recognized Willis Schultz and the other two men that had been with him in McIntire's General Store on the day they had given Chloe trouble.

"So we meet again," Willis said as the three men stopped, blocking the road.

"It would seem so," Gideon replied.

"But you don't have that buckskin clad, old goat to cover your back today."

Gideon pulled back his coat to reveal his badge. He kept his eyes on the men's hands as he did so. All of them had their wrists crossed, resting on the saddle horns. "No, but I got the law with me now."

"I don't think the law will do you much good if you are found dead with a bullet through that tin star," Willis said with a sneer on his face.

"Maybe not, but my partner would be smart enough to figure out who did it. Jack would kill all of you," Gideon said as he rubbed his scar.

"That old codger don't scare me."

"He should," Gideon said as he sunk his spurs into his horse. Rowdy lurched forward as if he were shot from a cannon. He crashed into Willis's horse, taking the mount and its rider to the ground. Gideon spun Rowdy around, drawing his revolver as he did so. The other men were too stunned by what had just happened even to have contemplated going for their weapons. Willis let out a scream as his horse rolled to his feet and stood, leaving the rider on the ground with one foot caught in the stirrup.

Fearing that the horse would bolt and drag Willis away to his death, Gideon said, "Grab the reins of his mount."

The rider to Gideon's right did as he was told.

As Gideon pulled back the hammer on his Remington, he said, "Gentlemen, I want you to very slowly remove your gun belts and toss them on the ground. You too, Willis."

Willis let out a moan. "I think my leg is busted."

"That has nothing to do with what I just told you to do. Now do it or I'm going to have to shoot you," Gideon warned.

Willis struggled to remove his belt while lying flat on his back with his foot still in the stirrup, but succeeded with the task. The other two men also complied with the instructions.

"Good. Now throw your rifles to the ground. Grab Willis's while you're at it," Gideon ordered.

After the men had obeyed the directive, Gideon climbed down from his horse. He retrieved the revolvers and shoved them into his saddlebag before grabbing up the rifles. As he climbed back onto Rowdy, he said, "Willis, the next time I have trouble from you, I will kill you. Do you understand?"

"This ain't over yet," Willis threatened.

"Considering the position you are in, I'm beginning to think that you're not a very smart man. I could take out my knife and slash some hide off your horse. You'd probably get dragged all the way into Ellsworth before it stopped, and I don't imagine there'd be much left of you."

"Sheriff Whitney is going to hear about this."

"I think you should do that. I bet you were a tattletale in school, too. Good day," Gideon said as he nudged his horse into a trot.

The optimistic mood that had buoyed Gideon earlier that morning had vanished into a cavern of despair. It seemed to him as if he attracted men of Willis Schultz's ilk like an oil lamp attracted bugs on a hot summer night. He could also feel his self-loathing creeping over him. Sometimes, he wondered why he bothered to put himself through the slog of living, and pondered if a real man would just end it.

Gideon held Rowdy to a trot all the way back to town. His plan to concentrate on how to solve Teddy's murder had faded away like a sunset. As he rode down the main street, he spotted Chloe walking on the boardwalk. He wasn't in the mood for talking, and acted as if he didn't see her.

"Good morning, Gideon," Chloe called out.

Letting out a sigh, Gideon turned his horse toward the voice. "Hey, Chloe."

Even though she barely knew Gideon, his sagging shoulders, and slack face all but shouted to her of his lowly state of mind.

"What's wrong with you? I saw Jack, and he said that you were raring to go prove Pa innocent. You look like you've lost your best friend," Chloe said.

"On my ride, I encountered Willis and his buddies. That man holds a grudge and could ruin the best of days."

"Did they hurt you?"

"No, I'm fine, but Willis may have a broken leg. He'll be out for revenge for sure now. Where are you headed?" Gideon asked to try to change the subject.

"I'm sorry that you keep getting dragged into my problems. I bet you wish you had never ever entered our store."

"It doesn't matter. Trouble would have found me anyway – it always does. And I wouldn't have a job if I hadn't impressed the marshal with my handling of Willis and that gambler."

"I suppose, but I would just as soon not be the reason for your employment. To answer your question, I have an appointment to see Youngston Bryant. He's the best lawyer in town," Chloe said.

"Good. I hope he can help your pa. A lawyer can probably get more done than a deputy like me ever thought about doing. I need to go put up Rowdy. I'll be seeing you," Gideon said, tipping his hat before riding away.

Chloe watched Gideon trot down the street. She had come to the conclusion that he was a much more complicated young man than most of the ones she came across in the cow town. He seemed to have a sweetness and intelligence to him, and a big, dark rain cloud over his shoulder.

She resumed her walk to the lawyer's office. Mr. Bryant had a reputation for being a crusty old curmudgeon. Chloe had learned that for herself firsthand that morning when she had been waiting at his office door for him. He had sent her packing with the instructions to come back at ten o'clock. Some people claimed the reason Mr. Bryant was so successful in his practice was that if a trial wasn't going to his satisfaction, he'd draw out the proceedings for so long that the judge would acquiesce to the lawyer's demands just to get the whole thing finished. Chloe was so determined to help her pa that she didn't care how Mr. Bryant treated her as long as he did his job.

"Good morning, Miss McIntire," Mr. Bryant said as he greeted Chloe at the door. He managed a small smile as he led her from the lobby to his office in the back.

The lawyer was in his fifties with wild curly hair that had already turned white and a bushy mustache that covered his top lip entirely. Mr. Bryant always attired his lanky frame in a long-tail black suit with a crisply starched white shirt. He seemed to have an endless supply of colorful ties that completed his ensemble.

As Chloe gazed around the room, she couldn't help but be impressed. The walls were lined with imposing looking leather-bound law books. His chair was high-backed and covered in premium grade red leather that matched the two chairs for clients. A massive desk made of mahogany occupied a large portion of the room, resting on the plushest carpet in which Chloe had ever sunk her feet. The thought crossed her mind that saving her pa might financially ruin them.

"Thank you for seeing me," Chloe said as she took a seat.

"I assume this is concerning your father being arrested yesterday for murdering Teddy Calhoun. Did Sean do it?" the lawyer asked in his typically blunt manner.

"No, of course not. Pa was with me the whole time. The only way he could have committed murder was to sneak off in the middle of the night, and I assure you that he did not."

"Why did they arrest him then?"

Chloe explained what had happened the day before the murder and the lack of evidence.

The lawyer pounded both of his fists onto the desk, causing Chloe to jump.

"Pardon my language, Miss McIntire, but that damn marshal is a grandstanding fool. I don't know why the mayor doesn't fire his ass. Happy Jack is going to get this town sued if he is not careful, and this could be the case that does it. That man seems to be oblivious to due process."

"I didn't know what to do. We should have come and seen you yesterday," Chloe said.

"Yes, you should have, but that is neither here nor there. You go on back to the store and let me take care of this," Mr. Bryant said as he stood and walked around the desk. He held out his hand and graciously helped Chloe from her seat.

"Thank you, Mr. Bryant."

"You are quite welcome. That's why I am here. Don't you worry yourself. I will take care of you and Sean – you can count on that."

The lawyer waited until Chloe was gone before dashing off in his long strides to the mayor's office. He barged into the room, catching the mayor reading the newspaper. Mayor Buford Cole was a short, middle-aged man with a protruding belly and a balding head. Mr. Bryant stood directly in front of the desk so that he towered over the mayor.

"That damn fool marshal of yours has arrested Sean McIntire for murder without any evidence," Mr. Bryant blurted out.

"Youngston, calm yourself. I'm sure Marshal Morco wouldn't have made an arrest unless he thought Sean did it," Mayor Buford Cole said.

"Thinking he did it and having evidence for an arrest is night and day."

"You know I try to stay out of the marshal's business," the mayor said.

"It's going to be your business when I sue the city for false imprisonment after the grand jury refuses to bring this to trial," the lawyer threatened.

"There's no call for that. I heard that Sean beat Teddy up the day before the murder. That certainly raises suspicion."

"If Sean McIntire planned on killing Teddy, he would have done it then. He's not the type to sneak in and do it in the middle of the night. Sean is too honorable of a man for that."

"What do you want me to do?"

"Buford, you are always talking about wanting to make Ellsworth a civilized place and not just another cow town. That can't happen as long as the marshal is arresting one of our finest citizens just so he can say he solved a murder. I've told you what I will do and I mean it," Youngston said before turning and leaving the mayor without so much as a goodbye.

The mayor slung his newspaper off his desk. "Damn lawyers. We ought to hang the whole lot of them," he muttered before leaving his office.

Marshal Morco was exiting his office when the mayor approached him.

"You need to release Sean this moment," the mayor barked.

Happy Jack stretched his neck back and furrowed his brow. "What?"

"You heard me. I'll not have you arresting people willy-nilly."

"That isn't your call, mayor. I'm the marshal."

"But as mayor I can fire you and I will do it on the spot if you do not release Sean this minute," Buford threatened.

"I still plan to bring this to the grand jury," the marshal said as he straightened his posture to look more commanding.

"That's fine, but you will not keep a man imprisoned without evidence. Get off your ass and prove he did it if that is what you believe," Mayor Cole said and walked away.

The marshal turned around and went back into the jail. He grabbed the cell keys and unlocked Sean's cell. "You are free to go until the grand jury decides whether to bring you to trial," the marshal said. He tossed the keys onto his desk and left the jail.

Sean scratched his head and raised his eyebrows. "I'd love to know the story behind that," he mused.

Chapter 9

Gideon had little time to ponder the state of his life after his run-in with Willis Schultz. By noon, word had spread that the first herd of cattle had arrived at a destination a couple of miles south of town. They would be grazing there until the beef fattened back up from the long journey from Texas. The women in Ellsworth were scurrying about buying groceries in hopes of avoiding getting out of the house for a few days. Merchants were busy stocking shelves, giddy with nervous energy over the expected boon to business coming their way.

Marshal Morco was pacing in his office when Gideon and Jack walked into the jail. The sound of the door closing caused the marshal to spin around on his heels. His eyes were livid with anger and his face was scrunched up in a scowl. He shook his finger at Gideon.

"Were you the one that talked the mayor into releasing Sean?" the marshal asked in an angered voice just short of yelling.

As Gideon glanced toward the empty cell, he said, "The only time I've talked to the mayor is when you introduced us to him. I've never even seen him again, and I didn't know Sean had been released."

"Well, it's a good thing. I won't tolerate my deputies undermining me. Chloe probably hired Youngston Bryant as Sean's damned lawyer. That silver-tongued devil could talk the skirt off a nun. Have you found any more evidence on who murdered Teddy?"

"Not yet, but we're still trying," Gideon answered.

"I guess I better get busy looking, too. I thought you'd have found something by now. Seems I can't count on anybody. Was your only job in Boulder to arrest the town drunk? What are you two doing in here anyway?"

Ignoring the rebuke, Gideon said, "Word is that a cattle herd is outside of town. We figured we'd be dealing with some wild cowboys in short order. How do you normally handle them?"

"Really? I guess I need to quit stewing in here and get out on the street more. As long as those darn cowboys aren't shooting their guns or tearing up the place, I let them do as they please. Try not to shoot them – it's bad for business. Most of them couldn't hit the broad side of a barn with a pistol anyway."

"One more thing. While I was out for a ride, I had another run-in with Willis Schultz. He may have a broken leg, and he's not a happy man."

"Neither am I. He can join the crowd. If you have to kill him, make sure you have some witnesses," the marshal said.

"Maybe it won't come to that. I guess we had better get out of here. I imagine we'll be having company any minute now," Gideon said.

"Well, don't let the door hit you," the marshal said before plopping down into his chair and tossing his hat to the floor.

Once outside, Jack said, "I'm surprised you didn't quit on the spot. I'm beginning to think that Happy Jack is a bit of a misnomer."

"I would if it wasn't for Sean. I'm not about to let him get railroaded for the murder," Gideon said.

"Having a conscience can be quite the burden, can't it?"

Gideon let out a little snort. "Something like that, I suppose. Let's go see Sean before all hell breaks loose around here."

Sean McIntire stood behind the counter waiting on a woman when the men walked into the store. He smiled and gave a little wave. When the customer left, he said, "I hope you boys aren't here to arrest me again."

"No, but we had to suffer the wrath of the marshal over your freedom. Happy Jack he ain't," Jack said.

With a chuckle, Sean said, "Yeah, sometimes the name really fits the marshal and sometimes it's all sarcasm. That man does run hot and cold. I do appreciate all the work you two have put into this, and I really hope you find the real killer."

From the office, Chloe recognized the voices and came walking to the front of the store. "Are you in any better frame of mind than when I saw you this morning?" she asked Gideon.

"Sure, I'm ready to dance a jig waiting for the cowboys to hit town," Gideon said wryly.

"You probably need a good meal before you do that. I've been so busy doing the books that I forgot to eat. Does the offer of lunch still stand?" Chloe asked.

Caught unprepared for Chloe's proposal, Gideon looked over at Jack as if he might have the answer.

"Don't look at me. Last I checked, you were a big boy," Jack said.

The tease caused Gideon to color. "Oh, shut up. Nobody asked you a thing."

"If you say so," Jack said, clearly enjoying the rousting.

"Chloe, let's get out of here. We both probably spend too much time in the company of old men," Gideon said as he took Chloe by the elbow and led her from the store, leaving Jack and Sean grinning at each other.

The couple walked to the café and took a seat at a table away from the other diners. The flirty waitress didn't seem to appreciate Chloe's presence, but put up a cheerful front nonetheless. They both ordered sandwiches. Chloe chose pork while Gideon selected beef.

"So, Mr. Johann, tell me a little about your past life," Chloe said with a disarming smile.

Gideon proceeded to tell her of his life in Last Stand, his time in the war, and some of the places he had worked since then.

"Do you go home often?" Chloe asked.

"I've never been back."

"Why not? I bet you still have friends there – and a girl you left behind."

Gideon rubbed his scar and puffed up his cheeks before loudly blowing out the air. "You ask a lot of questions. I just never saw a reason to go back."

Chloe gazed into Gideon's deep blue eyes. They had a sadness to them even when he dropped his guard and enjoyed himself. She had no doubt that there remained a whole lot more to his story than she would ever pry out of him. "So how did you get that scar that you rub when you are agitated?"

Letting out a grunt, Gideon touched the scar. He had never realized he did such a thing when he felt unsettled. "A Reb tried to split my head in two with his saber. He came mighty close to succeeding. Let's talk about you for a change."

Sensing that she had pried into Gideon's life as far as she was going to get, Chloe talked of her childhood in Fort Leavenworth and the family's move to Ellsworth. Something about being with Gideon made her feel like talking about her mother. She got downright chatty reminiscing about all the things they used to do together.

All the talk of Chloe's mother made Gideon uncomfortable, and he caught himself reaching to rub his scar. The conversation stirred up too many memories of his own mother and threatened to crack open all the bottled up emotions he never allowed himself to feel. To his way of thinking, no good ever came from looking back – just keep moving forward.

Fearing the conversation would turn back to his own life, Gideon asked, "How come you've never married?"

The question caught Chloe off-guard and felt condescending. She sat back in her chair, folded her arms across her chest, and peered at Gideon. "I didn't know I needed a man to make my life complete. Or maybe I've never met one that I thought was worth my love. I could ask the same question of you."

Gideon smiled and met her glare head-on. "I didn't mean to rile you. I just figured a pretty thing like you with your sweet personality would have more suitors than you could shake a stick at."

The compliment made Chloe giggle in spite of her irritation. "You are a sly one trying to get back on my good side with a little flattery. Maybe a little too precocious for your own good. But seriously, have you looked around this town? There's way more quantity than quality."

"You have a point there. I guess I'd better get back to work before I get into any more trouble. Happy Jack seems about as impressed with me as you do right now," Gideon said as he stood.

"Oh, I won't hold this against you. You are a man after all and I've come to expect little from them," Chloe said, grinning like a Cheshire cat.

"That's a smart philosophy. Don't expect much and you never get disappointed," Gideon said as he helped her from her seat.

They returned to the store, finding Jack and Sean playing a game of checkers. After Sean won the final game to take the best of three, the two deputies left to patrol the street.

"So how was your lunch?" Farting Jack asked.

"About like the rest of my day. I've managed to rile Willis Schultz, Marshal Morco, and Chloe McIntire, and it's just two o'clock. Should make for a great evening," Gideon replied.

"The way Chloe looked at you didn't strike me as someone that was mad. I think she's smitten by you – God knows why."

"I don't know why she would be either. I think she's smarter than that – at least I hope so."

Gideon's comment made Jack instantly regret his teasing. Throughout his life, he'd known a good many men that loathed themselves for the evil lives they had lived, but he'd never known anybody besides Gideon that hated himself and yet tried to live an exemplary life.

"I wish I could knock some sense into you. If I thought it would work, I'd whup you up one side of the street and down the other. You're too young to be so world-weary," Jack said.

Shaking his head, Gideon said, "Let's just go do our job. I'm not about to listen to either one of us yap about all that again."

A short while later, the calm of the town was interrupted by six cowboys riding at a hard gallop down the street with their pistols a blazing. They yanked their horses to a stop in front of the Cowboy Palace and reloaded their guns before resuming the mayhem by the discharging of their weapons.

Gideon and Jack made it down to the saloon about the time the cowboys had emptied their revolvers again. The deputies stood in front of the entrance and waited as the riders climbed from their horses.

"We're all for you boys having some fun after a long drive, but you need to keep those revolvers in their holsters and not tear up the place. It would be a shame to waste your wages on damages," Gideon said in a congenial tone as the men approached.

"Ah, we were just having some fun and announcing our arrival. We don't mean no harm," one of the cowboys said.

"Well, you succeeded. Now do me a favor and do as I ask. You'll save all of us a lot of grief that way."

The biggest of the men stepped forward, towering over Gideon and Jack.

"And what if we don't want to?" the tall cowboy asked.

"Then you will make my job hard," Gideon replied.

"There's a lot more of us than there are of you. If you know what's good for you, you'll go help little old ladies cross the street and leave us be."

"Listen, big fellow, I'm just trying to do my job and save you from getting in trouble. You can have your fun. Just don't be a nuisance," Gideon said, still trying to be conciliatory.

The first cowboy grabbed the arm of the tall one. "Quit trying to cause trouble. The deputy is just doing his job," he said.

The tall cowboy jerked his arm free and stared at Gideon. "I think you're just scared. Now scurry away before I whip you in front of the town."

With a loud sigh, Gideon drew his revolver and crashed it into the man's groin. The cowboy let out a groan as he doubled over in pain. Gideon shoved him to the ground and hopped onto his back. After grabbing the man by the hair with both hands, Gideon began rubbing the cowboy's face into the boardwalk while Jack pulled out his revolver and pointed it at the other cowboys.

"Now are you going to behave or do I have to rub all the hide off your face?" Gideon yelled.

"Stop. Stop. I've had enough."

Before standing, Gideon retrieved the cowboy's gun. "Boys, I really wanted to play nice, but your friend didn't give me much choice in the matter. Keep an eye on him and don't make me come back here." He handed the revolver to one of the other men before he and Jack walked away.

"You can be a mean little bastard when you want to be," Jack said once they were out of hearing range of the cowboys.

Gideon chuckled. "I just figured I'd make a statement now and maybe it would save us from having real trouble later."

"Or we will have that giant come looking to kill us."

"I doubt that. Those big ones aren't used to tasting their own medicine. It tends to take the fight all out of them. If this is the start of cattle season, I hate to think what the finish of all these cowboys coming to town will be like."

"You're liable to make too many enemies to ever get hired onto one of these trail crews if they are all like today," Jack said.

"Yeah, today hasn't been a good one for making friends. It'll teach me not to wake up in a good mood for sure," Gideon said.

Chapter 10

Fortunately for Gideon and Jack, the newly arrived cowboys minded their manners for the rest of their first evening in town. The deputies were able to head home after midnight once all the saloons' customers began to slink away for the night.

In the morning, Jack went with his brother to the hat shop while Gideon resumed his quest to find Teddy's killer. With all that had gone on the previous day, Gideon never had had an opportunity to talk to anyone else about the crime. He feared if much more time elapsed, that memories would grow dim on what witnesses may have seen on the night of the crime. While walking around town, he would stop everyone he met and ask the person if they could remember seeing anything unusual on the night of Teddy's murder. Nobody seemed to have seen a thing.

As the morning wore on, Gideon found himself trying to come up with an excuse to visit the general store. He wouldn't admit to himself his reason for wanting to go there, but instead kept thinking that he needed to check on Sean. With all the walking he had done that morning, breakfast hadn't stayed with him, and he latched onto the idea of going to get some jerky to hold him over until lunch.

The sight of the store crowded with customers had Gideon contemplating turning around and leaving. He had hoped to find business slow enough that he could loiter for a while without being a nuisance. Chloe looked up from the customer she was helping and gave him a smile. Her gesture made him decide to stay, and forced him to admit that he really did like being in her company. With no hope of getting to talk to Chloe or Sean anytime soon, Gideon went to fetch a package of jerky.

"What are you looking for, Mr. Johann?" Chloe called out from two aisles over.

"I'm a little hungry and thought I'd get some jerky," Gideon replied.

"If you are not in a big hurry, wait and I'll have something better for you."

Smiling, Gideon said, "I think I can fit you into my schedule."

For the next fifteen minutes, Gideon perused practically every item in the store until at last the crowd had cleared.

Sean, sensing what was happening, said, "Chloe, I'm headed to the post office. I'll be back shortly."

"Where's Jack?" Chloe asked.

"He's down at the hat shop with George. For somebody that claimed to never be close with his brother, they're like two peas in a pod these days," Gideon answered.

"I made an apple pie and brought it to the store. I figured you and Jack don't get home cooking very often and might like a piece. Us old maids have lots of time on our hands for baking and such."

"I never called you an old maid."

"You might as well have. You certainly insinuated it."

Gideon looked up at the ceiling and blew his cheeks up before exhaling. "Women."

"Come on back here," Chloe said as she headed for the office. She cut a generous portion of pie and put it on a plate before handing it to Gideon.

He sat down and cut his first bite. The crust was light and fluffy, and reminded him of his momma's pie. He took his first bite and chewed slowly. "Oh my goodness, I haven't had a pie this good in years. Actually, not since my momma died. You are one fine cook."

The lavish praise caused Chloe to beam with pride. Her grin lit the room. "Thank you. My momma taught me how to bake."

"Well, you certainly learned well."

"You'll have to tell Jack to come by for a piece."

"I could take it to him."

Chloe giggled. "Mr. Johann, I don't think I trust you that much."

"Ah, not only are you a good cook, but a wise one, too."

"Or maybe just distrustful."

Gideon took another bite of pie, turning serious as he chewed. "How is your pa holding up?" he asked.

"He's doing pretty well, I think. I heard him get up last night and pace around the kitchen for a while, but he has a lot of confidence in you solving this whole mess."

"That may well be misplaced trust. I haven't come up with anything yet," Gideon said before taking another bite.

"Pa has taken a shine to you. He fancies himself a fair judge of character, and truth be told, I guess he is. Please don't give up on him," Chloe said as she watched Gideon devour his last morsel of pie.

Gideon sat back in his chair and rubbed his belly. "Don't you worry about that. Of course, I may require a pie or two as my just reward when this all is said and done."

"That you can count on."

"Thank you for the dessert. That was mighty thoughtful. I best be getting back to work. I guess I'll send Jack your way since I can't be trusted with pie, but can be with your pa's future."

"Thank you, Gideon. Be careful," Chloe said as she stood.

"You take care, Chloe."

Gideon left the store and walked to the jail. Inside, he found the sheriff standing in front of the marshal, tying a string tie onto the lawman. The sight caused Gideon to squeeze his lips together to keep from grinning at the proceedings.

"What do you want?" the marshal asked gruffly in his embarrassment at having been caught needing help with his attire.

"I just thought I would check in with you. What's going on?" Gideon asked.

"We're headed to Teddy's funeral. We figured it best we be there to show we haven't forgotten about his murder. Anything new?" Marshal Morco asked.

"Not on the murder. I got into a scrape with one of the cowboys yesterday."

"I heard about that. Sounds like you handled things about right. Most of those boys will mind their manners once they find out they can't walk all over you. Willis Shultz came in here walking with a cane, and raising hell. His leg's not broken, just bruised up some. I asked him what started the trouble, but he didn't want to talk about it. He just wanted to tell me how you knocked down his horse. That was right smart thinking on your part. I do like the way you think."

"Desperation will make a man resourceful," Gideon said.

Sheriff Whitney finally had the tie fixed to his satisfaction. He turned to face Gideon. "You best keep an eye out for Willis. He's not one to dally lightly with."

"Yes, sir. I plan to do that."

"Do you need anything else?" the marshal asked.

"No, but I can fix your hair for you if want some more help getting prettied up," Gideon teased as he headed for the door.

"Boy, you better get the hell out of here before I accidently shoot you," the marshal yelled.

As Gideon walked past the grocery store, he heard a voice call out, "Are you a deputy?"

Gideon turned to see a small, older woman coming out of the building. "Yes, I am. I'm Deputy Gideon Johann. May I help you?"

"I'm Mrs. Lenora Jenkins," the woman said as she shifted her package from one arm to the other. "I just learned of the murder we had in town. I saw something that night that I think you should know about."

"Let's step over here and get out of everybody's way," Gideon said as he took the woman's package and moved away from the door with her. "Now tell me what you saw."

"I saw that saloon owner, Lonnie Wilson, walking down our street with blood all over his shirt."

Gideon eyed the woman, wondering if she might be making up a story to get attention. "What time was that?"

"It was two in the morning. I remember looking at the clock."

"What were you doing up at that time that you would have seen Lonnie?"

"Our momma cat and some old tomcat were making enough noise to raise the dead. I went outside and threw water on them."

"I see. Are you sure you got a good enough look to identify a person at that time of night?"

Mrs. Jenkins straightened her posture and pursed her lips. "Young man, I can see just fine with my spectacles on. Everybody that has lived in this town any time at all knows who Lonnie is. He walked right under a streetlight. I know what I saw."

"Did he see you?"

"I don't think so. I was standing in the dark and Lonnie was making tracks."

"And where do you live?"

"Herman and I live on the street behind the Cowboy Palace on the corner directly behind the saloon."

"Ma'am, are you confident enough about what you saw that you would testify to it under oath?" Gideon asked.

"I am."

Handing the package back to Mrs. Jenkins, Gideon said, "Thank you, ma'am. You've been a big help. I'm sure I'll be talking to you again."

"That will be fine. Nice to have met you, Mr. Johann."

Gideon rushed to the hat shop, finding Jack in deep concentration as he shaped a hat.

"You'll be trading in those buckskins for suits before long. Beaver will never have to fear your traps again," Gideon teased.

"Oh, shut up. I'm just passing the time. I'll be plenty good and ready to head home once I'm done babysitting your sorry carcass," Jack replied.

"Come on. We need to talk to Lonnie Wilson again."

Jack handed the hat to George and followed Gideon out the door. As they strolled toward the saloon, Gideon filled the mountain man in on what he had learned from Mrs. Jenkins. The Cowboy Palace had just opened for business, and the two deputies walked into the saloon to find Rosie, Trella, and Delaware already flirting with the early drinkers.

"Where's Lonnie?" Gideon asked.

Rosie let out a giggle. "I know you're really here to see me, aren't you, baby?"

Gideon was so intent on talking to Lonnie that the teasing failed to embarrass him. "I need to see Lonnie now," he said sternly.

"He's through that door there," Trella said, pointing to a doorway beside the bar.

"Thank you, ma'am."

Gideon led the way into the back room. Lonnie was taking inventory of his liquor. He glanced up, squeezing his lips together as if he expected an unpleasant visit with the law officers.

"We need to talk," Gideon said.

"Sure, what can I do for you?" Lonnie asked as he looked at Gideon and then toward Jack.

"I need you to tell me where you were on the night that Teddy was murdered."

"I already told you all that," Lonnie protested.

"The truth this time."

"What do you mean?"

"Damn it, Lonnie, we have a witness that saw you out on the street," Gideon said.

Lonnie Wilson's shoulders sank so much that it appeared as if he were shrinking. He looked down at his feet. "I still didn't kill Teddy. The truth is I went to pay a visit to Lisa Young. If you don't know her, she's a fine looking widow woman – a lonely widow. I go see her sometimes."

"You got out of bed with Delaware to go see Lisa?" Gideon asked incredulously.

"Delaware was so high that she wasn't any use to me. It's not like she's my wife."

"What about the blood?" Jack asked.

The question caused the color to drain from Lonnie's face. "Who was looking out their window at that time of night?"

"We'll ask the questions," Gideon said.

"I hadn't been at Lisa's place very long when Phillip Tyrone showed up. I guess Lisa shares her bed with him, too. He didn't appreciate me already being there, and we got into a fight. I bloodied his nose. Then I got him in a headlock and his blood got all over my shirt. That's the truth."

"So Lisa and Phillip can corroborate your story?" Gideon asked.

"They can if they tell the truth, but I don't know how likely that will be. Phillip is married. His wife is out of town while her sister has a baby. I doubt that Lisa will be too thrilled to tell the town that she shares her bed with more than one man. She has a reputation to protect," Lonnie said.

"This town seems to have its share of bed-hopping," Jack said.

"Show me a town that doesn't," Lonnie said with a snicker.

"This would sound a lot more believable if you had told the truth in the first place," Gideon reminded the saloonkeeper.

"Yeah, I guess I should have, but I didn't think I'd get caught. No matter how it looks, I didn't kill Teddy. I certainly had no reason to after all this time."

"Where can we find Phillip and Lisa?"

"Phillip is a big deal at the bank. I think he's a vice president or something. Lisa's house is two streets behind the Red Rose. It's white and faces north with all the flowers in the yard," Lonnie replied.

"I hope they back your story, Lonnie," Gideon said before leaving.

Out on the street, Jack said, "I don't know about you, but I think I believe Lonnie."

"You're the one that didn't believe him the first time and you were right. Now you think he's telling the truth? I don't know. If he is lying, he's sure good at coming up with a story on the spot. I guess we'll find out shortly," Gideon said.

The men entered the bank and marched up to the counter. A man of medium height with a thatch of jet-black hair and a pleasant face stood on the other side. He looked to be in his thirties and to have led an easy life.

"I need to talk to Phillip Tyrone," Gideon said.

"That would be me," Phillip said as he eyed the deputies suspiciously.

"Can we step outside for some privacy?" Gideon asked.

"I suppose."

Phillip followed Gideon and Jack outside and around to the side of the building.

"Mr. Tyrone, I need to know where you were two nights ago when Teddy Calhoun was murdered," Gideon said.

Phillip's eyebrows shot up and he rubbed his chin. "I don't know what this is about, but I spent all evening at my home. I'm a happily married man and I do not go frequenting the saloons."

Gideon studied Phillip's face trying to see if he could see any signs that the bank teller had been punched. If he had been on the receiving end of a blow, there didn't look to be any visible damage.

"We heard that you went to visit Lisa Young and got into a fight with Lonnie Wilson. Are you sure about your story?" Gideon inquired.

The bank teller set his jaw and his face reddened in anger. "I don't know who you think you are making such an outlandish statement, but I do not appreciate it for one moment. I do know both of those people. They are customers of the bank, but that is as far as my acquaintance with them goes. I will be talking to the marshal about this."

"Mr. Tyrone, I'm just trying to do my job. Your account of your evening could get a man hanged," Gideon said.

"I only know how I spent my evening. Anything else will be on somebody else's shoulders. Now I have a job to do. Good day," Phillip said before darting away.

"I seem to be doing a better job of making enemies than I do friends in this town," Gideon mused.

"I thought you did that in every town," Jack said to lighten the mood.

With a snort, Gideon said, "Probably so. Let's go hear Lisa's tale."

Lisa Young lived in tidy white clapboard house with roses growing all along the foundation. As the lawmen walked up, she was in the yard pruning the bushes. When she turned to face them, Gideon was surprised by her youthfulness. Lisa was probably no older the he was. She had long blond hair that she'd tied into a loose ponytail, and a beautiful face with steely green eyes. Gideon could imagine that a lot of men wished to pay the widow a visit.

"May I help you?" she asked.

"Ma'am, I'm Deputy Gideon Johann and this is Deputy Jack Dolan. We have some questions for you, if you don't mind."

Lisa looked at the men warily. "Sure," she said.

"Did you have any visitors to your home two nights ago? It would have been the night that Teddy Calhoun was murdered," Gideon said.

"It is very rarely that I have visitors in the evening. In fact, I can't recall the last time I had someone at the house after dinner."

Gideon glanced over at Jack. The old mountain man refused to make eye contact, and Gideon realized that he was on his own.

"Ma'am, it's really important that we get to the truth. Are you sure that Phillip Tyrone and Lonnie Wilson didn't visit you that night?" Gideon asked.

Lisa crossed her arms and pulled her shoulders back. "Mr. Johann, I'm not sure what you are insinuating, but I am a widow with a reputation to uphold. I certainly do not have men coming over to my home in the night. I would be the talk of the town. I do know Phillip from the bank, but I only know Lonnie Wilson by name. Your questioning is offensive."

"Thank you, ma'am. I'm just trying to do my job to make sure an innocent man is not arrested. You have a good day," Gideon said.

As they walked away, Jack asked, "How do you feel about all this?"

"Probably not as good as I should. Phillip and Mrs. Young sure shot holes in Lonnie's alibi, but they also have reasons to hide the truth and they both seemed to be offended awfully easily," Gideon said.

"It does seem odd that Lonnie would make up a story involving those two if there was no chance they would back him up," Jack mused.

"That's what troubles me, too. The marshal can decide what to do."

"An arrest is sure a lot easier when somebody is standing there with a smoking gun."

"That it is. I liked the way you stayed out of the conversation with Mrs. Young."

"I was just admiring the roses," Jack said with a grin.

"Did you see any of those colors that you claim surround people when we talked to Phillip or Mrs. Young? That way we can know if they are evil or not," Gideon asked half in jest.

Jack wrinkled up his face so that one eye was barely open. "I should have never told you about that. You're just making fun of me, but no, I didn't get the impression they were bad."

"I just wondered. I'd take any help I could get at this point. By the way, I guess I should tell you that Chloe has a piece of pie waiting for you at the store. It's to die for," Gideon said.

They strolled to the jail and waited for Marshal Morco to return from the funeral. An hour later, the sheriff and marshal arrived back at their office.

"What are you two doing loitering in here?" the marshal barked.

Gideon reiterated all that had transpired concerning Lonnie Wilson.

"I don't know what you're waiting for. He sounds guilty to me. Go arrest Lonnie," Marshal Morco ordered.

Chapter 11

If Sean McIntire's arrest for the murder of Teddy Calhoun could be considered a lesson in grace and quiet dignity, Lonnie Wilson's arrest would be remembered for being the completely opposite behavior. Gideon and Jack were forced to literally drag the saloonkeeper from the Cowboy Palace, kicking and screaming, while protesting his innocence. At one point, Gideon almost had to pull his revolver and waylay Lonnie as he nearly escaped the deputies' grasps. The whole town came to a standstill as the townsfolk watched the proceeding with fascination.

After jailing Lonnie, Gideon left the jail with his mood sinking like a rock in a lake. In his limited experience as a law officer, he had never before encountered an investigation where there was any doubt to a person's guilt. But this time, Gideon had no idea what to make of Lonnie's alibi. He couldn't imagine the saloonkeeper coming up with such an elaborate story that could be so easily disproved if it were a lie, nor could he grasp that two people would endanger another man's life merely to hide their secret tryst.

Jack could see from Gideon's dour expression that his young friend was struggling with the arrest and in no mood for levity. The mountain man thought about giving Gideon some time alone, but nixed the idea with a nagging fear that an irrational act by the deputy could happen at any moment.

"Why don't we go tell Sean the news? I can get my pie, too," Jack said.

"You can go on by yourself. I think I'll just keep on eye on things," Gideon replied.

Tugging on his long beard, Jack thought for a moment before saying, "Nah, I can wait."

Gideon managed a smile. "What's the matter? Are you afraid Chloe has eyes for old mountain men and you might not be safe alone with her?"

"I'm only fifty-five years old. Quit acting as if I'm as old as Methuselah. I don't feel near as old as my age may sound to you."

"I'll go with you. Somebody your age doesn't have many pies left in their life."

Chloe sensed the change in Gideon's disposition the moment he came through the store's doorway. His eyes no longer had the glint of merriment from his morning visit. Instead, she saw a troubled, lost-looking gaze. She found the transformation in Gideon unsettling.

"I see that Gideon did tell you about your piece of pie," Chloe said to Jack.

"Yes, ma'am. With his high praise, I didn't want to miss the opportunity," Jack said as he pulled off his hat.

Gideon looked over at Sean and said, "We just arrested Lonnie Wilson for the murder of Teddy. You should be able to rest easy tonight."

"Why, thank you, Gideon. I must admit that I do feel as if a burden has been lifted," Sean said.

"Why are you in such a dark mood then?" Chloe asked before realizing the tone of her question.

The inquiry caught Gideon by surprise and he grimaced at the realization that Chloe could read his disposition so easily. He started to rub his scar, but caught himself. "I knew your pa was innocent. With Lonnie, I'm not sure either way with him. He could be guilty or he could be a victim of circumstance. I'd prefer to know for sure."

"Oh, I see. I could imagine how such responsibility would weigh on you. Maybe another piece of pie will sweeten your outlook. You and Jack come on to the back. Pa and I don't need that much of it," Chloe said as she headed toward the rear of the store.

As Jack ate his pie, his gushing flattery of the dessert caused Chloe to blush in embarrassment and giggle like a schoolgirl. Even Gideon set aside his worries to heap on praise, causing Chloe to accuse the men of fibbing just to get her to bake more often. Sean came into the office to join the others in eating a slice of pie, and went so far as to suggest that if Chloe would bake more, she might catch her a man. The statement earned Sean a dirty look from his daughter that seemed to all but threaten him with his life if he did not hush.

The deputies finished eating and left the store. As they were walking down the street, the cowboys from the herd returned to town. They rode down the street in a fast trot, but none of the men brandished their revolvers. A couple of the cowboys even gave Gideon and Jack a little wave.

"What do you think the odds are those cowboys can behave themselves for another night?" Jack mused.

"I don't know," Gideon said, brushing off the question.

"Gideon, lighten up. They haven't hanged Lonnie yet. Let the law run its course before you get all down about this. He more than likely killed Teddy anyway."

"I suppose."

"What are you looking at?"

On the other side of the street, Gideon saw Lisa Young walk into Haley's Dry Goods.

"I just saw our Mrs. Young go into that store. I'm going to run over and talk to her neighbors while she's not home. I don't want her to know I was snooping around behind her back," Gideon said before jogging away.

Gideon approached the house on the left side of Lisa Young's home and knocked. An old woman cracked the door and peered out.

"Who is it?" she asked in a weathered voice.

"Hi, ma'am. I'm Deputy Johann. Can I ask you some questions?"

The door opened enough that the woman's ancient head appeared. "What is it?"

"Did you hear or see anything two nights ago? Teddy Calhoun was murdered that night," Gideon said.

"No. No, can't say that I did. Things stay pretty quiet around here. You visited Mrs. Young earlier today, didn't you?"

"Yes, I did. I was under the impression that she might have had a visitor that saw something, but I found out she isn't in the habit of receiving visitors in the evening," Gideon said in hopes of baiting the woman into talking.

The old woman let out such a cackle that Gideon immediately recalled stories from his childhood of witches.

"I don't know about that night, but don't let Mrs. Young fool you. She has menfolk pay her visits – sometimes late in the evening."

"Do you know any of her visitors?" Gideon asked.

"Nah, I never get a good look at them. At that time of night, they're just shadows, but they are men – that's for sure."

"Thank you, ma'am. I appreciate your talking to me. You have a good day," Gideon said before leaving. He took the long way back so as not to encounter Mrs. Young if she were returning home.

After tracking down Jack, Gideon said, "I talked to a neighbor lady. She didn't see or hear anything, but Lisa Young does have men pay her visits."

"That doesn't surprise me, but it doesn't prove anything either," Jack replied.

"It proves she lied to us."

"But that's all. We can't refute her or Phillip Tyrone's story without a witness that says otherwise. Let it go for tonight and sleep on it. Let's get some food. By the time we're done eating, those cowboys will be getting liquored up," Jack said.

Jack's reaction to the news miffed Gideon. He grew sullen, following the mountain man to the café without saying anything further. They ate their meals while barely carrying on any conversation.

With the Red Rose shut down because of Teddy's demise, and the Cowboy Palace closed after Lonnie's incarceration, the other saloons in town were doing brisk business. Gideon and Jack tracked down the cowboys in the Dusty Trail Saloon. The whores from the Cowboy Palace had already taken up residence there also. The deputies managed to get a table where they could keep an eye on the card games. Burton Rochester, the gambler, was playing poker at a nearby table with three of the cowboys from the trail herd. He gave the deputies a little wave as he sneered at them.

Back when Gideon worked as a deputy in Boulder, Sheriff Howell had made a point of taking his new hire to the saloons to teach him how to spot cheating in all the various games played by the patrons. Gideon planned to put the training to good use that night. He kept his eyes trained on the gambler, waiting for him to deal from the bottom of the deck or pull a card from his sleeve.

Rosie, the whore who had teased Gideon at the Cowboy Palace, brought two beers to the table. She made a point of bending over as far as possible to show-off her cleavage. With a giggle, she said, "Hey, blue eyes, my offer still stands. I can show you a mighty fine time. There's nothing like a redhead in bed."

Gideon was in no mood to be embarrassed or to put up with the flirty whore's annoying banter. "The only thing I might want from you is another beer. Now get away from me before I think up a reason to throw you in jail."

The rebuke seemed to actually hurt the whore's feelings. She scurried away without saying another word.

Jack took a drink of beer and set his mug down loudly. "Gideon, ease up. She was just playing with you. That's how she makes a living. I doubt she grew up wanting to be a whore. That's just where life took her."

"If you think I can be hard on a whore, wait until I catch that gambler cheating. I'll make him wish we had never crossed paths," Gideon said.

"Don't forget that you are representing the law," Jack reminded him.

Gideon scowled before taking a drink of beer. He resumed his watching of the gambler, furrowing his brow in concentration. If Burton Rochester noticed, he never gave any indication. After the game had gone on for a while, Gideon came to the conclusion that the gambler had no need to cheat when playing cards with the cowboys. Burton only needed skill at his profession to beat the rubes at the table.

One of the cowboys stood up abruptly, sending his chair scooting across the floor. "I smell a cheat," he yelled as he stared at Burton.

"I'd think real hard about what I was about to say if you are thinking about accusing me," Burton said in a calm, measured tone.

Gideon scrambled to his feet and started moving toward the card table. "Cowboy, you haven't been cheated. You're just bad at cards," he hollered.

The cowboy made a wobbly turn toward the voice. "And who the hell are you?"

"You already know I'm a deputy. You need to calm yourself down before you get hurt," Gideon warned.

"Sit down, Lou," one of the others pleaded.

Lou went for his gun. Gideon was ready for him. He drove his fist into the cowboy's jaw, throwing his whole body into the punch. The cowboy dropped as if he had been hit with a shotgun blast. Gideon pounced onto Lou's stomach. He intended to release the rage that had been building in him all day upon the helpless cowboy. As Gideon drew back his fist to pound Lou's face, he found himself yanked away. He spun his head around to see Jack dragging him.

"Gideon, you knocked him silly. You can't beat a helpless man," Jack said in a tone of authority.

Gideon glared at Jack as he got to his feet. He didn't say anything, but turned and stormed out of the saloon.

Jack pointed his finger at the cowboys still sitting at the table. "You boys take your friend and get on back to your herd or I'll throw you all in jail. You've had enough fun for one night. Deputy Johann saved your friend's life," he said before heading out to find Gideon.

Gideon was pacing in a circle underneath a streetlamp. He'd tossed his hat onto the ground and rubbed his hand through his unruly hair until the strands were standing in every direction. His face looked as if he was deranged. He spun to face Jack when he heard the footsteps coming his way.

"Jack, don't you ever do something like that again," Gideon yelled.

"You need to calm down, but I'll do whatever I need to do to keep you from doing something you'd regret," Jack said.

"I can do whatever I want. I don't need you looking after me," Gideon screamed.

"Son, the reason I came to Kansas and why I'm still here is that I've seen trouble simmering in you for a couple of months. I'm trying my damnedest to look out for you."

Gideon raised his fist. "You want to see trouble. I'll give you trouble."

"Hit me if it'll make you feel better, but I won't raise a hand to you. You're my friend. I'd be dead if not for you," Jack said quietly.

As Gideon dropped his arm, he fell to his knees. His shoulders began to shudder and a sob escaped his lips. "Jack, I'm sorry. Sometimes I'm so miserable. I saw and did things in that war for which I can't forget or forgive myself. It gets the best of me," he blubbered out nearly indiscernibly.

"Gideon, we've had this talk before. You don't do you or anybody else any good by not forgiving yourself. The world has enough misery without you adding to it. If you think you need to pay for your sins, do it by being happy and making life better for those you meet."

"Don't you see? I need to be miserable. That's all I deserve."

Jack shook his head and tugged on his beard. "I pray there comes a day when somebody comes into your life that will help you. I truly believe that will happen one day, but unfortunately, I don't guess it will be me. You need the love of a woman. Go on back to George's house and get to bed. You're in no condition to work. I'll be along when the saloons slow down for the night."

"Jack, you're a good friend. I haven't had one since the war. Thanks for looking out for me."

"You've done the same for me. That's what friends do. Now get going."

Chapter 12

The smell of bacon frying aroused Jack from his slumber. He glanced over at Gideon, lying next to him. His young friend looked to be in a deep sleep, likely exhausted from his behavior and the stress of the previous day. Jack crawled out of bed and headed to the kitchen. The first thing he noticed upon entering the room was an empty whiskey bottle sitting on the table.

"Looks like your friend drowned his sorrows last night," George said as he looked over his shoulder from the stove.

"Yeah, he had a bad day yesterday," Jack conceded as he sat down at the table.

"I like Gideon, but he sure seems to be a moody sort."

"He's got some demons chasing him and he doesn't know how to handle them."

"Why do you care so much? You were never one to look out for others," George said as he carried a plate of bacon and a bowl of scrambled eggs to the table.

Jack glanced up with a puzzled look upon his face, wondering to what his brother was referring. "If you are talking about us, I always had your back. You just don't remember the times I stood up for you. We might not have been the closest of siblings, but nobody got away with picking on my little brother."

"Maybe so, but I sure don't remember it. Seems like I always got picked on in school."

As Jack scooped out a generous helping of eggs, he said, "Not when I was around you weren't. The trouble was that momma always babied you and you were soft. Bullies go after the softies."

"You could have helped me be tougher," George said as he filled his plate.

"I did try, but you'd go run to momma and tell her I was being mean to you. It was hard teaching you to fight without popping you once in a while."

George let out a little chuckle. "I did bloody Johnny Call's nose one time. He left me alone after that."

"You turned out just fine – with or without me," Jack said.

"I shouldn't have said anything. I'm just thankful we've gotten to spend some time together again after so long apart."

"Me too. As for Gideon, he saved my life when I barely knew him. It was a miracle that he didn't get himself killed in the bargain. That buys a whole lot of loyalty in my book."

"I'd say it does," George said, talking with a mouth full of eggs.

The men finished their breakfasts and left the house to head for the shop, leaving Gideon to sleep away the morning. He finally woke up a little before ten o'clock. As he crawled out of bed, he took stock of how he felt. Amazingly, he didn't feel hungover. He ambled into the kitchen and fixed himself some breakfast. Afterward, he pulled out the tub and heated water. Once he finished giving himself a thorough scrubbing, Gideon shaved and put on a clean change of clothes. He looked out the window into the bright light and smiled. A memory crossed his mind of his momma saying that the sun always came up the next morning no matter how bad the day before had seemed.

Gideon was in no hurry to meet up with Jack. He felt embarrassed by his behavior toward his friend and wasn't anxious to face him. Strolling into town, he vacillated between going for a ride and seeing Chloe. Truth be told, he wanted to pay her a visit. It had been a long time since he had enjoyed the company of such a fine girl. As he headed toward the store, his mind raced for an excuse to go inside the business. He walked in still wondering what he'd say.

"Good morning, Mr. Johann," Chloe said with a big smile from behind the counter.

"Good morning to you. Is Jack in here?" Gideon asked. The question seemed to come out of his mouth without his brain ever having considered such an excuse for being in the store.

"No, I haven't seen him this morning. I thought you two were joined at the hip," Chloe said. She gave an impish grin. Her intuition told her that Gideon knew full well that Jack wasn't anywhere near the place.

"I'm lucky enough to get away from him once in a while. I fear I'll pick up all his bad habits."

"I bet you have plenty of bad habits to go around as it is. On the other hand, you certainly look all spruced up."

"I just took a bath and shaved."

"It becomes you," Chloe said mischievously.

Gideon rubbed the palm of his hand against his chin and grimaced as he wondered if Chloe was making fun of him. "It's not like I go around smelling like a pig," he said defensively.

"I was just teasing. You're awfully sensitive for somebody that bucks up against bullies."

"Oh. I guess I've just gotten out of the habit of dealing with sassy women."

"But I bet you had plenty of practice back in the day. I was wondering if you might like to go for a ride and a picnic this Sunday. We could take Pa's delivery wagon. I know a perfect spot," Chloe said.

"Uh, I don't know. I hadn't really thought about it," Gideon said, surprised by the proposition.

"Well, of course you hadn't thought about it before I even asked. What kind of thing is that to say? Just forget it. I thought you might like to spend some time in the company of somebody different for a change. You can just go ahead and sit around all Sunday afternoon with musty smelling old men for all I care."

Gideon held up his hands as if he were trying to keep a heifer from charging. "No, I'll go with you. I've just never had a woman ask me out before now. I was a bit taken aback."

"You don't have to if you don't want to go on a picnic. I'm not begging you or anything. I wouldn't want to offend your sensibilities of how a female should behave," Chloe said.

"I look forward to the picnic."

Sean walked into the store. "Oh, hello, Gideon."

"Pa, Gideon is loitering in here and keeping me from getting any work done," Chloe said, her tone as serious as a preacher.

The storekeeper looked at his daughter and then at Gideon. The deputy was turning red and seemed at a loss for words at Chloe's accusation. Sean knew his daughter well enough to realize that she would have already run Gideon out of the place if he were really a nuisance.

"We better be nice to him. He might arrest me again. Maybe he'll buy something the next time he's in here," Sean said, giving Gideon a wink.

"Meet me here in front of the store at noon on Sunday," Chloe commanded.

Gideon shook his head in dismay and then gave a little salute before walking out of the store without saying another word. He tried getting his head around all that had just happened. In all his years, he couldn't recall ever dealing with such a perplexing woman. He wasn't sure if Chloe liked him or just enjoyed torturing his poor soul. As he strolled down the boardwalk, he smiled. The whole exchange had been kind of fun.

Figuring he'd avoided Jack for as long as possible, Gideon headed toward the hat shop. As he walked up to the store, he saw Jack sitting outside on a bench, smoking his pipe. Gideon opened his mouth to speak, but couldn't find the words to say what was on his mind.

Jack rolled onto one ass cheek and let out a thunderous fart. "Whoa, that was a good one," he said.

Gideon snickered. "You're really a disgusting old goat."

"Pretty much."

"Jack, I'm sorry. My behavior was inexcusable."

"We're just fine. We all have bad days. Come sit down with me," Jack said before taking a puff on his pipe. With a thoughtful looking expression, he blew out the plume of smoke.

"I think I might let the air clear a little first," Gideon said, grinning again at his friend's crude way of extending an olive branch.

"It already has, my friend. It already has."

Chapter 13

On Sunday morning, as Gideon readied himself for the picnic, Jack and George teased him relentlessly for bathing and shaving again so soon. He hurriedly dressed in freshly laundered clothes, and left the house wearing his gun belt and carrying his Winchester 1866. On his way over to the store, he'd managed to pluck some flowers from the garden of one of George's neighbors. Gideon made sure to arrive a little before noon for fear of suffering Chloe's rebuke if he were to be late.

Chloe walked up a couple of minutes later toting a picnic basket and a blanket. She had dressed in a dark skirt with matching vest, a white blouse, and riding boots. A big brimmed hat covered her head.

"Here are some flowers for you," Gideon said as he held out the bouquet and tried not to stare. Chloe looked stunning. Her outfit showed off her fine figure a whole lot more than the usual dresses she wore to work.

"Why, thank you. You didn't steal them, did you?" Chloe teased.

Gideon grinned. "I might have borrowed them from someone's garden."

"That's a fine example for a deputy to make. I suppose it's still a nice gesture nonetheless."

"You look nice. I like your hat," Gideon said.

Placing her hands on her hips, Chloe looked down at herself. "You are quite the gentleman today. I see you've spruced up. Your face is liable to get sore from shaving so often."

"I think you like to give me a hard time."

"Just trying to keep you humble. I wouldn't want that head to get too big. Do you really need your guns?"

"I don't stop being a deputy just because I'm on a picnic," Gideon said as he took the basket from Chloe.

"Fair enough point. We have to get the horses and wagon at the livery stable," Chloe said.

The couple walked to the stable, and Gideon helped Martin harness the horses. He tried to draw more information out of the young man, but learned nothing new. Martin seemed reluctant to discuss his past life.

As they rode down the main street of Ellsworth, Gideon said, "I still can't help but think I've met Martin somewhere before now. Do you know anything about him?"

"No, nothing at all. Ever since Ellsworth got the reputation for being a wild and woolly place, we have a lot of drifters show up looking to make their fortune. I'm not saying that is the case with Martin, but I wouldn't be surprised either," Chloe replied.

"Which way?"

"The picnic spot is to the north. I'll show you how to make a big loop and then we can stop."

As they rode, Gideon marveled at a countryside that looked as flat as flapjacks and had very few trees. The view brought back memories of riding through Kansas as a soldier, but he didn't let his mind linger on the war. More than anything, he felt homesick for the Colorado Territory. "Have you ever been out West and viewed the mountains?"

"No, I've only seen pictures. I would imagine the sight is a whole lot more majestic than Kansas."

Smiling, Gideon said, "I wasn't going to say that, but now that you mentioned it, yes it is. Those mountains will make a man realize that he is very small and not nearly as important as he'd like to believe. I love them. You should go see them sometime."

"Maybe I just will."

"You'd probably never come back to Kansas if you did."

"Why did you leave your mountains then?"

"I don't stay anywhere for very long. I like to keep moving. This is a big country and I figure I might as well see some of it."

"Are you running from something?" Chloe asked.

Gideon looked Chloe in the eyes before speaking. "Just myself," he said before deciding he should change the topic. "So what are your plans for your life?"

Chloe caught a flicker of pain flash in Gideon's eyes as he spoke. She knew he intentionally changed the subject and she didn't want to delve into something that he didn't want to discuss. "I've been trying to get Pa to buy some of the land around here. I keep telling him that land values will have to keep going up as more people settle in Kansas. He likes to hoard his money in the bank."

"A sassy woman with a head for business. A combination that should take you far," Gideon said.

"You are making fun of me," Chloe said.

"I most certainly am not. That certainly was by all means a compliment. I've always admired intelligent women."

"What is her name?" Chloe boldly asked.

Gideon let out a chuckle. "You make for some dangerous conversation. Her name is Abby."

"And where is Abby?"

"My guess is she's in some big city, married to a rich man, and has a bunch of children. Let's talk about something else. All of that happened before the war."

"I'm sorry for prying. Curiosity got the better of me. Momma always called me Nosy Chloe."

As the ride continued, Chloe decided to stick to safer subjects. She talked mostly about her childhood growing up in Fort Leavenworth. Gideon realized he needed to contribute to the conversation. He never mentioned the name of his hometown, but he did talk of his life on a small ranch. The two even strayed into a conversation about losing their mothers at a young age and the change it brought to their lives.

"Here's the spot," Chloe announced as they reached West Oak Creek. The stream was shaded by massive oak trees and carpeted in thick grass.

Gideon helped Chloe from the wagon, and as she went to pick a spot and spread the blanket, he retrieved the picnic basket and his rifle.

"I hope you like fried chicken," Chloe said as she retrieved the food from the basket.

"Everybody likes chicken as long as the cook knows how to fix it," Gideon responded as he sat down next to Chloe.

"I didn't hear you complaining about my pie."

"Good point."

Chloe opened a can of beans and set the chicken out before retrieving bread, plates, and spoons. They were both starving and wasted no time in filling their plates.

Gideon bit off a big chunk of meat from a leg. He chewed slowly, savoring the taste. All the while, he could see Chloe watching him and waiting for a reaction. "I'm not prepared to say your chicken is better than your pie, but darned if it isn't a close second," he said.

Grinning, Chloe said, "I'm never sure if you're sincere or just trying to stay on my good side."

"If I've tried to stay on your good side, I'd say I've done a pretty poor job of it. It's true that I would lie if it tasted bad, but this food surely gives me no reason for that."

"Thank you. I'm glad you like it."

After that, they barely talked as they ate. Chloe had to stifle a laugh as she watched Gideon devour the chicken. He could pick a bone as clean as a whistle. She came to the conclusion that he really did like her cooking. He would finish a piece, toss the bone into the grass, and grab another.

"Save some room for pie," Chloe warned.

"You made pie again? You're going to make me fat."

"You could stand to put on some weight. You look like a matchstick running around town," she said as she pulled out the pie.

"You don't lack for opinions on much of anything, do you?" Gideon asked.

Chloe had forgotten to bring a knife so Gideon pulled out his and wiped it in the grass a couple of times before cutting the pie.

"I probably don't want to know where that knife has been," Chloe mused.

"Probably not, but remember I'm eating with you so it's not too bad."

As they ate the pie, Gideon effused over it, going so far as to claim that it tasted better than the first one. Chloe would smile with each compliment until it got to the point of being embarrassing.

"Just eat. I believe you," she finally said.

After they finished eating, an awkward silence fell over them. Neither of them seemed to know what to do next.

Gideon ran his hand through his hair and absently rubbed his scar. "Chloe, I just want to make sure you understand that I won't be in Ellsworth for very long. That was never my plan. I don't want you to go thinking that I'm marriage material."

Chloe slapped her thighs and her eyes grew narrow as she squeezed her lips together tightly. "Gideon Johann, you are a vain man. I try to do something nice for you after all you did for Pa, and you accuse me of trying to corral you into marriage. What makes you think I'm so desperate to get married or that I would be interested in you if I were? I think you're trying to ruin a fine day."

"No, I'm not. I just don't want you to get the wrong impression is all. I'm trying to be honorable."

Shaking her head, Chloe realized that Gideon would be no easy catch. He was not the average cowboy that went around telling a girl whatever she wanted to hear. He was way too noble for that. Of all the men she'd met in Ellsworth, Gideon stood head and shoulders above them. Marriage really wasn't on her mind just yet, but she knew she sure wouldn't mind roping Gideon in for some courting. She decided a little sugar might be the best way to accomplish that. She said, "You could have fooled me. Now are you smart enough to slide over here and kiss me or not? A little canoodling never hurt anybody. I promise I won't take it as an impending engagement."

Trying not to look as dumbfounded as he felt, Gideon gazed at Chloe without changing expressions. He never would have imagined that Chloe could be so bold. It occurred to him that he somehow seemed to get mixed up with strong, outspoken females. Abby had certainly been no shrinking violet either. As much as he doubted the wisdom of the proposal, the sight of a willing pretty girl won out over logic.

Gideon scooted over and pecked Chloe lightly on the lips before pulling his head back to see her reaction. Chloe didn't hesitate in wrapping her hands around his head and pressing his mouth into hers. Much to his surprise, Gideon quickly concluded that Chloe McIntire sure knew how to kiss. They lost themselves in pent-up desires, kissing until their lips felt puffy. Gideon paused and gazed into Chloe's eyes. His needs were close to winning out over his conscience. He'd only had sex with one person he loved. All of his other experiences had been with whores. Chloe was certainly no whore, but he didn't love her either – at least not yet. A sudden sense that they weren't alone interrupted his thoughts. He grabbed his rifle and stood. Willis Schultz and his two men were riding their way.

"How does Willis show up every time I leave town?" Gideon wondered aloud.

"His ranch isn't very far from here. I guess I should have chosen a different location. I bet he spotted the wagon while out riding and is coming over to nosy around," Chloe said as she stood.

"That's close enough," Gideon yelled when the riders were about fifty yards from the wagon.

"Well, if it isn't my favorite deputy and store clerk out here on a little picnic. No wonder the deputy made such a show in the store," Willis called out.

"Willis, you and your boys best just get out of here and leave us alone," Gideon said and cocked his rifle to make his point.

"You're an awfully big talker. One of these days you're going to have to back up your words."

"I think I already have twice now. If you come one step closer, I'll make it three times."

"You're lucky you didn't break my leg. I still owe you though," Willis said before turning his horse and riding away with his ranch hands following him.

"We better head back to town," Chloe said.

"No, not yet. We'd be out in the open if they tried to come after us. We need to wait them out and make sure they're not sneaking back. I could defend us from here," Gideon assured her.

"Surely he wouldn't try to kill us."

"I don't think he would harm you, but I have no doubt that he'd be coming if I were alone," Gideon said as he looked up and down the creek. He walked to the water and found a place he liked if they needed to take cover. "If I tell you, run and jump into the creek at this spot."

Gideon stayed on guard for over a half hour before deciding they could head back to town. "Can you drive the wagon?" he asked.

"Sure. Pa taught me how before I could climb onto the thing."

"Good. I can be ready for trouble that way."

The couple hastily loaded the picnic basket and blanket before setting out for town. Gideon stood in the back, constantly checking every direction for riders coming their way. He didn't let his guard down until they made it back to town without incident.

"That was certainly the most exciting picnic I've ever been on," Chloe said as they reached the livery stable.

"Me too, and things were pretty exciting before Willis showed his face," Gideon said, giving a wink.

Chloe playfully slapped Gideon's arm. "Hush."

After the horses and wagon were put up, Gideon said, "Thank you for the picnic. All things considered, I had a nice time."

"Me too. I had better get home. I will need to start supper for Pa before long," Chloe said before giving Gideon a quick kiss.

"Goodbye. I might have to look for Jack at your store tomorrow," Gideon joked before walking away.

On the stroll back to George's place, Gideon tried to get a handle on all that had gone on that afternoon. He felt surer than ever that a day of reckoning was coming with Willis Schultz. When that day came, he planned to be ready. As for Chloe, he didn't know what to make of the situation. He knew he liked her a lot, but he seriously doubted he would ever have the ability to love a woman again. And even though he had not seen Abby in years, the idea of having feelings for someone else felt like cheating. Then his mind jumped to wondering if Abby ever still thought about him. By the time he reached the house, he wished he'd never flirted with Chloe in the first place. Paying for whores seemed to be a much simpler way to live one's life.

"So how was your picnic?" Jack asked.

"Exhausting," Gideon said as he plopped into a chair.

Chapter 14

Without consciously making a decision to do so, Gideon more or less took the same course with Chloe that he had with all those he had been close to back in Last Stand – he avoided her at all cost. He didn't go into the general store, and when he neared the place, he made a point of walking on the other side of the street. His behavior wasn't the result of no longer wanting to see Chloe – he just didn't have the wherewithal to deal with the long dormant feelings stirring ever so slightly in him that she brought forth. Jack tried to talk to him about the newly developing situation, but gave up in frustration when he got nowhere with the conversation.

Gideon departed the hat shop at noon to get something to eat. He was restless and edgy, and decided not to invite Jack because of it. Sometimes it felt good to be alone for a while. He walked to the grocery and ordered a boiled pork sandwich at the meat counter.

As he waited patiently for his order, a voice from behind him said, "You don't have to avoid me if you don't want to go on any more picnics. I could handle the news. I am a big girl. I'm not sure I could say likewise about you."

Gideon turned to see Chloe glaring back at him.

"Can we step outside and discuss this?" Gideon said before glancing over his shoulder. "I'll be back for my sandwich."

Chloe made a beeline for the front door with Gideon following at her heels. She walked outside and headed to the side of the building without giving him a chance to catch up to her.

She spun around as if she were about to be attacked from behind and asked, "What do you have to say to me that you couldn't have said inside the grocery?"

The look Gideon got reminded him of a cornered mountain lion. He could imagine Chloe showing her teeth and extending her claws. "Chloe, please calm down. I know I should have paid you a visit by now, but I couldn't make myself. When I don't know how to deal with something, I just avoid the situation. I'm sorry. That's just me," he pleaded.

"So a man that's brave enough to fight in a war, be a deputy, and never back down from a fight, is scared to deal with his feelings? Is that why you don't know where your Abby is and why you don't ever go home? How does running help anything?"

"I just didn't want to lead you on to expect more than I can give. I know where this could lead and I know I'll run. My life hasn't been lived working behind a counter in a store. I have a past that you don't know about and never will. I'm not who you think I am."

The air seemed to deflate out of Chloe and her posture sagged as she exhaled loudly. She met Gideon's gaze head on, and her voice came out soft and without rancor. "No, Gideon, the problem is that I know you better than you know yourself. I know exactly who you are now. You still want to believe in whatever happened in your past. Sometimes living with the skeletons in the closet is easier than moving on with your life. They've become your mistresses." She turned and walked away before Gideon could respond.

Gideon went back in the grocery, and with a chagrined expression, retrieved his sandwich. He paid his money and stomped outside, eating his meal on a bench. By the time he took his last bite, his mood had changed from one of embarrassment for getting called out to that of frustration for his handling of the whole thing. He had to concede that Chloe had been spot on in some of her observations, but a lot of it, in his opinion, had been clueless and pure conjecture on her part.

With his mood in shambles, Gideon ambled over to the jail. Sheriff Whitney and Marshal Morco were sitting at their desks carrying on a conversation when he walked into the office. Gideon poured a cup of coffee, and took a seat in a chair along the wall. He slouched in his seat and stretching out his legs.

"What's wrong with you?" the marshal asked.

"Oh, I'm fine. Just relaxing," Gideon answered.

"I just got word that the grand jury bound Lonnie Wilson's case over for trial. We'll just have to wait for it to get on the docket. You did some good work on that one," Marshal Morco said.

"Did I? I know Sean didn't kill Teddy, but I'm only half convinced that Lonnie did it. I fear the two people that could collaborate Lonnie's alibi are more worried about protecting their reputations that they are his neck."

"That's for a jury to figure out. You did your job. Lonnie certainly had motive. Teddy made sure the whole town knew that his partner had swindled him. It just took Lonnie a long time to get his revenge," the marshal said.

From outside, the racket of a barrage of shots interrupted the quiet, sounding as if a battle had erupted. The men jumped to their feet to see what had happened.

Farting Jack came flying into the office. "I was just on my way over. Looks like a new bunch of cowboys have just hit town," he said excitedly.

"Everybody grab a scattergun. Seems like we have to put the fear of Jesus into every new crew that hits town," the marshal lamented.

The four lawmen marched down the street toward eight cowboys. Most of the men were riding in a circle and firing their guns. A couple of the riders raced down the boardwalk, sending bystanders scurrying for safety.

"You boys need to put your guns away and calm down before somebody gets hurt," Marshal Morco yelled at the top of his lungs to be heard over the gunfire.

All but one of the cowboys pulled his horse to a halt and stopped firing. A lone rider acted as if he didn't hear the marshal and kept circling his horse and shooting his revolver. The sound of breaking glass caused everyone to look toward the source of the noise. A figure standing in a hotel window slowly crumbled from view.

"Drop your gun and get off that horse or I swear I'll blow you out of the saddle," the marshal ordered.

The cowboy, realizing the precarious position he was in, did as he was told.

Gideon and Jack dashed toward the hotel. Once inside, Gideon recruited the desk clerk to grab his set of keys and come with them. The men bounded up the stairs to the room on the far left side of the building. As the clerk reached for the lock, his hands were shaking so badly that he could barely get the key into the hole and turn the tumbler. They burst into the room to find a little old lady sprawled on the floor. She had taken a bullet so squarely to the heart that the shot could have come from facing a firing squad.

"Isn't that the lady that has the seamstress shop?" Jack asked.

"Yup, that's Elisa Moore. I don't know why she wasn't at the shop. I didn't even realize she was still in her room," the clerk said.

Elisa Moore was a widow lady that had moved with her husband, Arthur, to Ellsworth several years back. Rumor had it that Arthur had become wealthy in Kansas City by some unknown means. He reportedly had wanted to come to Kansas to make his second fortune in the still young state, but Arthur died before he ever decided on his next business venture. The couple had no children, and Elisa decided she would remain in the town, taking up permanent residence in the hotel. She liked to sew and mingle with people so she opened her seamstress shop. Elisa had a reputation around town as quite the talker and for reciting any number of Shakespeare's sonnets without prompting. Children called her the Penny Lady. She seemed to carry an endless supply of pennies in her bag that she freely passed out to any and all children. The town liked to think of Elisa as their very own eccentric little old lady.

"There was no call for this. Those damn cowboys think they have to act like heathens," Gideon said.

"Yeah, and the town is going to be riled up good. Mrs. Moore was right popular. I guess I better go fetch the undertaker," the clerk replied.

Gideon and Jack headed outside as the clerk retrieved a blanket to cover the body. Sheriff Whitney and Marshal Morco were standing in the street with the cowboy they had arrested. From the looks of things, Gideon surmised that a bit of a standoff between the lawmen and cowboys was underway. The sheriff and marshal seemed hesitant to turn their backs on the horsemen to take the prisoner to the jail.

"He killed Elisa Moore," Jack called out.

"What a damn fool. You just killed the sweetest old lady in this town," the sheriff cursed.

"Gideon and Jack, get over here," the marshal ordered.

After the deputies joined to other two lawmen, the sheriff pulled back the hammers to both barrels of his shotgun. He made himself tall, and said, "Boys, I know you're wondering if you should help your buddy, but there's nothing you can do for him now. He's going to have to answer to the law for what he did. I don't know how good of shots you all are, but I know that if we have to unleash these scatterguns on you that there are going to be more of us still standing than you all still sitting in the saddle. Now you can either ride out of here and go back to your herd, or you can dismount and head to the saloons. Whatever it is, you had better do it now. My patience is wearing thin."

"Boys, let's go have a drink. Getting ourselves killed ain't going to help Carl," the oldest of the cowboys said.

The men proceeded to tie up their horses and walk toward the Dusty Trail Saloon. Once the cowboys had disappeared inside the establishment, the law officers walked the prisoner to the jail and locked him next door to Lonnie Wilson.

"I fear we're liable to have some trouble on our hands," Marshal Morco said as the men took seats in the office.

"That's what I was thinking, too," Sheriff Whitney said.

Gideon looked up at the surprising comments. "Do you really think those cowboys would try to break their friend out of here?" he asked.

"Maybe. I'm more worried that our citizens are going to be coming for the cowboy for a little lynching. Mrs. Moore's death is not going to sit well," the marshal answered.

"What do we need to do?" Gideon asked.

"We will all sit here and see what happens. If the cowboys come, we probably have a fighting chance, but if it's the townsfolk yielding shotguns – well that's a horse of a different color," Marshal Morco said.

"We can't just let them take him," Gideon protested.

"We are sworn to uphold the law, and I aim to try to talk them out of a hanging, but I have no intention of getting us all killed as we kill a bunch of our citizens to try to prevent it. There's no logic in that," the marshal said.

"Doesn't seem right."

Sheriff Whitney stood and looked out the window. "Son, you best listen to the marshal. You and Jack just follow our lead if something were to happen. We've been doing our jobs for a while."

To pass the time, Gideon lit the stove and made a fresh pot of coffee. He was in the process of filling all of the men's cups when the door of the jail burst open and about fifteen gun wielding, hooded men streamed into the room.

"We've come for the man that killed Mrs. Moore. We are fed up with these cowboys coming to town and tearing up things. They went too far this time. We aim to make an example out of the cowboy," the lead man said.

Before speaking, Marshal Morco took a sip of coffee as if he had nothing more pressing to do. "I know you're all upset – hell, we're upset too, but more than likely the judge will hang him anyway. Why don't you let the law handle this?"

"Because when word gets out that we hang cowboys that don't mind their manners, we'll begin getting a little respect around here. No disrespect to you and the sheriff, but you both have to follow the law when dealing with these heathens. We don't aim to this time."

Sheriff Whitney stood and faced the men. "You boys need to think about what you're about to do. I'd hazard a guess that most of you have never killed a man before, and you're also liable to give the town a bad name with the cattlemen. They could start going to a different town."

The leader of the vigilantes pointed his shotgun at the sheriff. "You know we don't want to hurt any of you. Take off your gun belts. We're going to lock you up until this is all over with."

Sighing, the sheriff reached for his belt buckle. "I think we better do as we're told." He unbuckled his gun belt and set it on the desk. Gideon, Jack, and the marshal did the same.

The leader grabbed the keys and unlocked the cell door. At the sight of the masked men coming his way, the cowboy began screaming and begging for his life. Four men dragged him, kicking and screaming, from the lockup. The leader made a motion with his head, and the lawmen walked into the cell.

"Somebody will let you out when our work is done," the leader said as he locked the door.

As the townsfolk hauled the prisoner outside, they were surprised to see his fellow cowboys walking down the street toward the jail. The cattle crew had consumed a sufficient amount of liquor to feel brave enough to go retrieve their friend. Seeing the hooded citizenry, armed mostly with shotguns and rifles, gave the cowboys pause. They stopped in the street and stood there like statues.

The leader of the townsfolk stepped forward and called out, "We're going to hang your friend. You best get back to your herd and make sure every cowboy knows that we're going to start hanging you heathens if you don't mind your manners. If I were you, I'd take off running now. At the count of three, we're opening fire on you."

As the vigilantes aimed their weapons, the cowboys took off in a mad dash for their horses.

"Should we shoot behind them to scare them real good?" one of the townsfolk asked.

"No, we wouldn't be setting much of an example if we did the same reckless thing those idiots did. Let's get this over with," the leader said.

The men lugged the cowboy to the nearest telegraph pole and threw a rope over it. Somebody fetched a barrel and set it upright under the noose. By that time, the cowboy had exhausted himself from thrashing about and pleading for his life. He accepted his fate and offered no resistance as they hoisted him onto the barrel. None of the men bothered to ask him if he had any last words. As soon as the rope was tied off properly, one of the men kicked the barrel out from under the cowboy. The drop did not break his neck. Nobody had thought to tie his hands, and the cowboy, his eyes bulging wildly, scratched at the noose as he kicked his legs violently.

"Grab his legs and yank," the leader ordered.

Two of the men managed to each secure a flailing leg. With nods of their heads at each other, they used their weight to pull on the cowboy. His neck snapped audibly and he grew still.

"Everybody needs to get back to whatever they were doing," the leader said before walking away.

A little while later, Rosie, the whore from the saloon, came into the jail and unlocked the cell. She didn't say a word, just tossed the keys onto the desk and left. The lawmen walked outside to the telegraph pole and stood there looking at the body swaying gently in the breeze.

"You had to know who some of those men were," Gideon said.

"Sure we do. I imagine between me and the sheriff, we could name you every one of them," Marshal Morco said.

"Aren't you going to do something?" Gideon asked.

"Sometimes the law takes care of the town. Sometimes the town takes care of the law. It's best to know when to let things be. This is one of those times. You and Jack need to get that body down," the marshal said before turning to go back to the jail.

Chapter 15

As Gideon sat for breakfast on the day after the hanging, he said, "I didn't get the impression that the sheriff or the marshal were all that bothered that the vigilantes hanged that cowboy."

"No, I was sitting here thinking the same thing," Jack replied before cramming bacon into his mouth.

"It just doesn't seem right to me."

"So says the man that hanged a killer just before we got to this town."

Gideon gave Jack a hard look. "That cowboy yesterday proved to be a fool, but he didn't aim to kill Mrs. Moore. The man we hanged took part in deliberately killing a whole family. I'd say there's a big difference."

"All the same, we could have delivered that killer to the law and let them handle it."

"I get your point. You don't have to beat it to death. I just don't think a judge would have hanged that cowboy. Some prison time would have been enough. The men we tracked down definitely deserved to have their necks stretched," Gideon said before taking a sip of coffee and wishing he had never brought up the subject.

"I heard that Chloe dressed you down in the grocery yesterday," Jack said. He squeezed his mouth tightly shut to stymie a smile, but the merriment in his eyes gave him away.

Gideon nearly choked on his coffee. "Who told you that? That happened just before the cowboys came to town and I've been with you ever since then," he said.

"That's not the point. The point is mean old Gideon let a girl tear into him. Boy, you got a lot to learn about women."

"Oh, listen to you – a man that probably hasn't been with a woman in a hundred years or more. But you're right. I riled her up but good. I got nobody to blame but myself for ever encouraging her in the first place," Gideon said.

"That girl would make a fine wife. She'd keep things interesting. I bet she'd even straighten you up," Jack said. He slurped his coffee as he watched Gideon, his eyes still twinkling.

Gideon ignored Jack, but noticed George eating his breakfast as if he didn't hear any of the conversation. It occurred to Gideon that when he had left the shop yesterday, George had been out running errands.

"George, were you the one spying on me?" Gideon asked.

George didn't speak, but his face gave him away as guilty.

"I'll be damn. The Dolan brothers have done me in. One is a little tattletale and the other is a busybody. I bet the next time I decide to pull up stakes and head somewhere new that I keep it to myself."

Jack burst out laughing, causing him to fart at the table. George got tickled and started giggling, too. All the merriment at Gideon's expense caused him to grab his hat and head for the door. As he walked outside, he could still hear the brothers carrying on like a couple of schoolgirls.

Gideon marched toward the general store. He wasn't sure why he headed that way. Maybe it was because of Jack's teasing. Maybe it was to make amends with

Chloe, or maybe he just wanted to see her again. Sean and Chloe were unlocking the door to the business as he stepped up onto the boardwalk. The loud clomping of his boots caused them both to startle and quickly turn their heads to see who was coming toward them.

"Chloe, may I have a moment of your time?" Gideon asked.

Chloe let out a sigh upon seeing they weren't about to be robbed. The sense of relief that came over her made her feel tingly as her heart pounded against her chest. "Sure," she said. Her father hastily slipped into the store without taking time to greet the deputy.

"Do you know how to ride a horse?" Gideon asked. He was so intent on his mission that it never occurred to him to ask her how she was doing or say some other pleasantry before launching into his purpose for being there.

"A little, but not very well."

"Would you like to go for a ride on Sunday? We could have the meal at the café beforehand so we don't starve while riding like last time."

"I suppose as long as you find me a gentle horse," Chloe answered. She wanted to smile as she watched Gideon's intensity. He didn't look much different from when he confronted Willis in the store on the day they'd first met. Only his pretty blue eyes kept him from looking harsh. They were the bluest eyes she'd ever seen. She decided she could look into them all day long.

"I'll see if Jack will let you ride his gelding. He's good and gentle. If it's all right with you, I'll meet you at your home at noon."

"All right. I had better get inside and help Pa get things a going. See you then," Chloe said before darting into the store.

The moment that Chloe disappeared inside the business, it dawned on Gideon that he had handled asking her out for a ride as if it were an inquisition. He smiled anyway. Having gotten the asking out of the way, he felt ready to meet the day head on.

∞

Chloe fretted from the moment Gideon asked her out for the ride on through watching out the window for him to arrive. She wondered whether he would expect her in a skirt and to ride sidesaddle – not that she had any notion to do such a thing. She just didn't want him to think her unladylike. Riding a horse in a skirt seemed just plain impractical, and her skills at riding were precarious enough without sitting sideways.

Mrs. Greely, the neighbor lady, helped her make a pair of riding pants out of stiff denim in time for the ride. The pants didn't fit perfectly, but they weren't bad. Looking at herself in the mirror, she had to admit that they showed off her figure a whole lot better than any dress ever had. She hoped Gideon would think likewise.

She spied Gideon ambling into the yard, and quickly moved away from the window. When he knocked, she counted to ten before going to the door – no need in him thinking she was anxious for his arrival.

Opening the door, Chloe playfully said, "Good day, Mr. Johann."

"Good day to you, Miss McIntire. I hope you are ready to go eat. I'm hungry," Gideon said as he gave Chloe the once over. Seeing her in pants was certainly a shock, but one that he didn't find at all unpleasant.

They walked to the café and took seats at the only table available. Gideon noticed other customers looking their way and talking. He wondered if the big news was seeing them together or the fact that Chloe wore pants. Either way, he kind of liked giving the townsfolk a reason to gossip. If Chloe observed the gossiping, she never let it show. The Sunday special was meatloaf, and both of them ordered it. The waitress returned shortly with the meat, browned potatoes, and cooked carrots.

"So where are we going to ride?" Chloe asked.

"I guess to the south. I've crossed paths with Willis twice now going north. I won't make that mistake again," Gideon replied.

Chloe looked Gideon brazenly in the eyes. "Does my wearing riding pants bother you?"

"No, I worried you'd wear a skirt and have trouble riding. I think the pants become you," Gideon replied.

The compliment caused Chloe to smile even as she tried to suppress it. "Thank you."

They spent the rest of the meal discussing the cowboy's hanging and the death of poor old Mrs. Moore. Both incidents had greatly upset Chloe. Gideon agreed with her, keeping his voice low when speaking his views of the hanging for fear of it getting back to the marshal or sheriff.

Afterward, Gideon and Chloe went to the livery to get the horses. The stable owner, Mr. Nance, waited on them. Martin Sanders, the young man Gideon still thought he'd known in the past, was nowhere in sight.

Gideon wondered if Martin had quit his job, but didn't ask. Mr. Nance wasn't one for much conversation.

Chloe tentatively climbed up onto the horse. The stirrups on Jack's saddle didn't even need to be adjusted to fit her, something that Gideon planned to tease the old mountain man about when the time was right. She sat there stiffly as Gideon mounted up, and then tried to get the horse to move as if asking its permission instead of commanding it to do so.

"Take charge of that horse like you do everything else or it will take charge of you. He's gentle but not stupid. Just pretend he's me," Gideon said with a grin.

Unable to resist the temptation, Chloe smiled and said, "You mean the part about being a gelding."

Gideon turned red and nudged his horse into moving.

Still smiling, Chloe took a breath and then followed Gideon's advice. She firmly squeezed the horse's sides and said, "Giddy up," in an authoritative voice.

The couple headed south. The terrain in that direction didn't really look any differently than any other direction around Ellsworth. Everywhere an eye could see was all flat. They came upon the Smoky Hill River and followed it southeast for a while. Across the river, they could see the two cattle herds that were fattening up before they would be driven into town. They kept on riding, deciding to avoid the cattle crews in case any of the cowboys were holding grudges against Gideon. They came upon a sandbar and tied up the horses. After pulling off their boots, the two of them walked barefoot in the sand and sat down on the trunk of a driftwood tree.

"This feels good. I can't remember the last time I went barefoot like this," Chloe said as she dug her toes into the warm sand.

"Me either," Gideon replied.

They sat there a good while without talking, content to take in the peacefulness of the place and enjoy each other's company.

Breaking the silence, Chloe asked, "So when you were a boy growing up, where did you see yourself at this age?"

Gideon sat for a moment thinking about his youth before speaking. "I was an only child and my friend, Ethan, had all sisters. We had all these plans to build a big ranch together. Both of our fathers were content to be smalltime ranchers and make just enough money to get buy. We planned on being rich together. Ethan was like the brother I never had."

"Sounds ambitious. And I bet you planned on marrying Abby," Chloe said.

"Yes, I guess I did."

"I bet there was no guessing about it. Why didn't you ever go back home?" Chloe asked.

Gideon looked at Chloe, trying to decide how to get out of answering the question, but decided that avoiding a response would be futile. "That war changed things. I didn't deserve those things any longer. What were your dreams?"

Chloe gave Gideon an inquisitive look, trying to decide whether to dig deeper about his war experiences before concluding that he would have told her more if he had wanted her to know such things. "I guess I thought I'd be married with a couple of children by now. Maybe staying home with them, and my husband working in the store with Pa."

"You'll have that someday, just not on the schedule you had planned. I'm sure of it," Gideon said.

"And will you have yours eventually, too?"

"No, I'm never going back to Last Stand. It's too late for all of that. Time has moved on for me. I lost everything when I got the fool-headed notion to enlist in that war," Gideon said as he picked up a flat stone and stood. He skipped the rock across the water five times before it sunk below the surface.

"We're a sorry sounding pair for two people that still have a lot of living to do."

"No, you're not. Your family just chose a bad town for you to reach your dreams. Me, I made my own mess," Gideon said as he turned to look at Chloe.

He held out his hand to her and helped her to her feet. They walked hand in hand the length of the sandbar, saying very little. The stroll gave Chloe time to reflect on the man by her side. She had no doubt that they had the makings of what it would take for a great love story, but sadly, she knew that that story would not come to be. There remained some deep, dark secret in Gideon that prevented him from being able to give his love freely. She also suspected he still held an allegiance to Abby that no other woman would ever be able to break.

"Gideon?"

"What?"

"Will you always remain my friend?" Chloe asked.

"That, Chloe, is something that I can give you – I promise."

∞

As soon as Chloe walked into the house after the horse ride with Gideon, Sean noticed his daughter's quiet demeanor. Her normally effusive personality seemed subdued and distracted. She said little and retired to her room until the time came to start supper. As she sat at the table peeling potatoes, Sean sat down across from her and lit his pipe.

"Do you want to talk about it?" Sean asked.

"Talk about what?" Chloe asked a little too innocently.

Sean snorted. "Don't insult me. You know what I'm talking about."

Chloe let out a breathy sigh and set her knife down on the table. "Pa, I'm falling in love with Gideon and it's all going to be for naught."

With a puff on his pipe, Sean blew out a plume of smoke with a thoughtful expression as he sought out what he wanted to say. "Don't sell yourself short. Sometimes you have to work for what you want. If I had given up on your momma that easily, you wouldn't be sitting here right now. I think the only reason she went on that first picnic with me was because she just plain got tired of telling me no."

"This isn't the same thing. Fact is, I think he fights what he wants to feel. Something bad happened when he fought in the war. I don't know what it was. He won't say, but he's consumed with guilt. I don't believe he thinks he's worthy of happiness."

Sean scratched his neck out of discomfort over where the conversation had turned. "Oh, I'm sorry to hear that. I never suspected that he was troubled. He always seemed like such a fine young man."

"Yes, that's what makes it so sad. He's so honorable that it hurts. I've never met anybody quite like him. When he lets the pain slip away, he's so sweet and kind. Those deep blue eyes just twinkle."

"Maybe I could talk to him," Sean suggested.

"No, he won't talk about it. I think he's too ashamed," Chloe said as her eyes started to well up and she made a quick swipe of the back of her hand across her nose.

"Now, don't cry."

"I can't help it. I feel so sorry for him. He's too good of a person to be so miserable. And the truth of it is, I'm crying for me, too. I'm going to end up an old maid and die with no family of my own. The old ladies around here already think I am one. I never dreamed I would end up alone, but this town is full of nothing but wild cowboys and scoundrels out for easy money."

Sean looked down at the table as he rubbed his forehead and puffed his pipe. "Maybe we should have never moved here. Money doesn't mean much if you're not happy. Margaret might even still be alive if we hadn't. We just never realized what a cow town would really be like before we came. And in my heart, I know we thought we had your best interest in mind."

"I know you did. Don't blame yourself. Maybe there's something wrong with me that scares all the good ones away," Chloe said, managing a sad smile.

"Don't say that. You are right – this town has slim pickings when it comes to upstanding young men. Chloe, we have enough money that I could send you back to Leavenworth. You could be near all your aunts, uncles, and cousins. I don't want you lonely."

"I'm not leaving you. We have a store to run. I shouldn't have said anything. I'm just sitting here feeling sorry for myself," Chloe said as she picked up her knife and resumed peeling the potatoes.

"You're a good daughter. I probably don't tell you that enough. And you're beautiful, too. You look more like your momma every day. A man would have to be blind not to want to chase after you. Don't you give up. I still believe the right one is out there somewhere."

Chapter 16

With Gideon's realization that Chloe had accepted the fact that she and he would never be more than friends, the young deputy found his reaction to the situation to be different from what he had desired. He still didn't regret that he had discouraged her from ever seeing any possibility of them being a couple, but found himself slipping into a deep loathing because his character made the relationship doomed in the first place. The notion that his past would always be every bit as much a part of him as the scar on his cheekbone made Gideon doubt that life was really worth living any longer. Spending time with Chloe had also opened up the old wound left by abandoning Abby. He had started thinking of her again, something that he never did anymore. Abby was undoubtedly married by now, and he hoped she had found happiness, but being around Chloe made him miss her all over again. He also was well aware that while no one would ever replace his first love, Chloe had all the makings of someone he could have a happy life with if he were capable of expressing that emotion again.

Gideon could barely will himself out of bed. He had slept little since the day of the horseback ride. Even copious amounts of whiskey were not helping in bringing some much-needed sleep. Stumbling into the kitchen, he saw that Jack and George had already eaten their breakfasts.

Jack had noticed Gideon's sinking spirit ever since the Sunday ride. He didn't know what had happened and knew better than to ask. Gideon looked like hell. He was dark under the eyes and his face looked puffy from all the alcohol. The whiff of whiskey clung to him as if he used it for cologne. What concerned Jack the most was that when Gideon got like this, he was trouble waiting to happen.

As Jack got to his feet, he said, "Let me fix you some breakfast."

"I don't know, Jack. I don't have much of an appetite. I'll take some coffee," Gideon said as he dropped into a chair.

"I'm fixing you some eggs and bacon. You don't need to get any thinner than you are or the wind will blow you out of the saddle. You'll feel better with some food in your stomach."

Gideon didn't have the will to argue with the mountain man. He looked up at Jack and nodded his head. "Sure." For all the grief they gave each other, he had to admit that Jack always looked out for him.

Jack busied himself with fixing the breakfast, humming as he worked. As the bacon began sizzling, he asked, "What are your plans for today?"

The question brought Gideon out of his reverie. He hadn't even thought about his intentions for the day, but without stopping to think, he said, "I think I'll interview Phillip Tyrone and Lisa Young again. Maybe their stores will change."

"So you're still not convinced that Lonnie Wilson is murderer?"

"Not really. I don't have anything else to do, and I don't feel like reading all day."

When the meal was cooked, Jack set the plate of food in front of his friend. Gideon took his first tentative bite, fearing fried egg might actually nauseate him, but found the food tasted good. He commenced eating as if he were starved.

"Don't get yourself into trouble," Jack said as he put on his hat. "I'll be at the shop if you need me."

"Not me," Gideon said with a mouthful of egg.

After finishing his breakfast, Gideon felt as if he might make it through the day. He looked at himself in the mirror, realizing he needed a shave, bath, and a change of clothes. Trouble was, he just didn't give a damn what people thought of his appearance. He strapped on his gun belt and strolled to the bank.

The bank had just opened for business. Phillip Tyrone stood behind the counter waiting for his first customer of the day. His eyes narrowed and he snarled his lips upon seeing Gideon headed toward him.

"What do you want?" Phillip asked.

"I need to talk to you again," Gideon replied.

"Mr. Wilson has been arrested for the murder of Mr. Calhoun. I have nothing left to say on the matter."

"You can either step outside with me or I'll ask the questions in here in a voice loud enough that everybody will hear me."

Phillip stormed around the counter and followed Gideon to the side of the building.

"What is it?" Phillip asked impatiently.

"I need you to tell me again where you were the night that Teddy was murdered. I want the truth," Gideon demanded.

"I already told you that I spent the evening alone at my home. My wife is back in town, and if she gets wind of this nonsense, I'll have hell to pay. She's not a trusting soul."

"I don't believe you."

"I don't care what you believe. You come into the bank smelling as if you bathed in a barrel of whiskey and look like you slept under a porch. I swear to you that if you bother me again, I will take my grievance to the mayor and get results. He likes me and he can make that marshal dance to his tune. Do I make myself clear?"

"So you're willing to let an innocent man hang to cover up your affair?" Gideon asked.

Phillip walked past Gideon without answering and went back inside the bank.

The encounter hadn't gone any better than Gideon expected it would, and truth be told, he figured he probably could have handled it better. But what it all boiled down to was that Phillip Tyrone wasn't going to change his story no matter how he was approached.

As Gideon walked to Lisa Young's house, he wondered how the young widow supported herself. If he had to guess, he would bet she'd been a whore that had snagged herself some rich old fart with one leg in the grave. Lisa answered the door in a housecoat. She smiled knowingly at Gideon as if she didn't seem surprised or even mind that he had returned. Her demeanor certainly seemed friendlier than their first meeting.

"What can I do for you, deputy?" Lisa asked as she looked past Gideon to see if he were alone.

"I wanted to ask you again about the night that Teddy was murdered," Gideon stated.

Grinning, Lisa said, "A lawman with a conscience – imagine that. I already told you I'm not in the habit of keeping company in the evenings. I'm afraid I can't help you."

"Ma'am, I know that you have men visitors in the evening."

Lisa burst into laughter. "You've been talking to that nosy old lady next door. I knew she's been watching me. Anyway, I didn't have any visitors on that night. That's just the facts."

Gideon rubbed his scar, wondering what to say. Finally, he said, "Thank you for your time."

"Deputy, now that you know I have the occasional visitor, why don't you come in for some coffee? I make it nice and hot," Lisa said with a mischievous grin.

"I think I'll have to pass," Gideon said before turning away.

The interrogations that morning had only created more doubt than ever in Gideon's mind that the real killer hadn't been arrested. The problem remained that he didn't have a clue on how to find out the truth. In his current state of mind, Lisa Young's seductive offer also seemed pathetic. He figured it took a sad and troubled woman to offer herself so freely to whatever man she could bed.

Gideon walked into the jail to find Marshal Morco in a loud argument with an older looking cowboy.

"You're lucky your whole darn crew didn't get strung up that day. People are tired of cowboys coming to town and shooting up the place," the marshal hollered.

"That still doesn't give them the right to hang a man. And I have a hard time believing that a bunch of hooded men came and locked you up and you didn't recognize any of them or that nobody saw where they went to afterward. They didn't just vanish into the air," the cowboy fired back.

"Well, I didn't, and nobody is talking. If you are so all concerned, why did it take you nearly a week to come look into the matter?"

"Because I wanted to let things calm down first. I feared I might suffer the same fate as Carl if I came too soon, and I wanted to wait and see if any arrest had been made. Obviously you have no intentions of arresting anyone for his murder."

"If I learn of any of the culprits, I will arrest them. You know, you're to blame for this. Those men work for you. If you laid down the law before they came to town or took their guns away from them, none of this would have happened. Nobody needs a gun to drink, play cards, and screw a whore," the marshal yelled before standing.

The trail boss stood and eyed the marshal for a moment before stomping out of the jail.

In an irritable voice, the marshal asked Gideon, "What do you want?"

"Not a thing. I just decided I would drop in for a moment," Gideon replied. He'd already decided that there was no point in confessing his concerns over Lonnie's guilt to the marshal.

"Oh. Good thing, because I've heard enough nonsense for one day."

"I sure hope that the hanging doesn't cause us more problems instead of setting an example," Gideon said as he stretched out his legs and crossed them.

"I doubt that will happen. The townsfolk put the fear of God into those cowboys and I expect word will travel that it's best to mind your manners in Ellsworth," the marshal replied.

"You know best."

The marshal studied Gideon a moment before speaking. "I know you probably think my nickname of Happy Jack is pure sarcasm, and I admit I've been a bit riled lately, but I don't mean to be. I probably should say it more – you and Farting Jack have done a good job around here and I appreciate your work. I've had deputies that weren't smart enough to get out of the rain. Thank you."

"I appreciate that. I guess I better get going," Gideon said and stood. Compliments made him uneasy, and he felt too restless to sit for long anyway.

He decided that maybe sprucing up would also improve his mood. He went back to George's house and bathed, shaved, and put on clean clothes. The lack of sleep made him feel as if his limbs had weights attached to them, and the warm bath had relaxed him to the point that he could barely keep his eyes open. He crawled into bed and fell asleep immediately.

By the time Gideon awoke, it was nearly two o'clock. He jumped out of bed and rushed out of the house. The nap had done wonders for his exhaustion though he couldn't' say it had done much for his mood. He hurried to the grocery to buy a boiled pork sandwich, and devoured it as he headed for the hat shop.

"Well, you look a sight better than when I last saw you," Jack said as soon as Gideon walked into the shop.

"I wish I could say likewise," Gideon replied in a tone devoid of humor.

"Doesn't seem to have improved your disposition."

"I'm fine. Don't be so touchy. Did you expect me to say thank you?"

"I'd settle for you not looking like you're spoiling for a fight."

"Are you ready to get to work? There's nothing else to do," Gideon said.

"Let's get busy then," Jack said as he grabbed his hat.

They spent the rest of the afternoon patrolling the streets of Ellsworth and then had a meal in the hotel dining room for the first time. As the sun sank to the west, twenty cowboys calmly rode into Ellsworth. Some of the men were from the first two crews that had previously come to town. The new faces were from a freshly arrived herd. All of the men wore revolvers, but none of them had their weapons out of their holsters.

"I wonder what tonight has in store for us," Jack mused as he and Gideon watched the riders dismount in front of the Dusty Trail Saloon.

"Maybe they'll stay on their best behavior for at least one night," Gideon said.

With the closing of the Red Rose and Cowboy Palace, the Dusty Trail had become the most popular saloon in town. Gideon and Jack slipped into the establishment just as darkness fell. They had to wrangle their way through a sea of cowboys and townsfolk to get up to the bar to order beers. The place was roaring with laughter and conversation, and smoky enough that one just needed to breathe to satisfy their tobacco cravings. Burton Rochester, the gambler, played cards with four of the cowboys and looked to be taking most of their money.

"I'm going to take the first chair that comes available when one of those cowboys loses all of his earnings," Gideon said.

"Do you think that is wise? We are working," Jack said before taking his first sip of beer.

"I don't see why not. If there's trouble in town, it will be in here. It doesn't really matter if I'm playing cards or standing at the bar when it happens. I can do my job either way," Gideon said.

Jack studied Gideon's face. He wondered if his friend planned to play cards for pleasure, or whether he might have designs on making trouble for the gambler. "I suppose," he finally said.

The first casualty of the card game happened a few minutes later. A cowboy cussed, threw down his cards, and jumped up from the table. Gideon slid into the chair before anyone else had the chance. He smiled and said, "Let's play cards, boys."

Gideon kept his eyes on Burton every time the gambler dealt. As the game progressed, he and the gambler were doing most of the winning. One cowboy was holding his own and the other two were losing badly.

During the war, cards were one of the main sources of entertainment in camp. Gideon had spent countless hours playing poker. He never could beat his friend, Finnie Ford, until the Irishman had finally taken pity on Gideon and told him why. Finnie informed Gideon that he always rubbed the side of his nose when he had good cards, and bit his lip when holding a losing hand. The news had been a revelation, and after that, Gideon made sure to keep a poker face.

Burton dealt Gideon four tens and a trey. As Gideon studied the cards, he felt as if he were being watched. He glanced up and caught the gambler looking at him. At that moment, Gideon realized he'd been distracted by Delaware, the whore, getting into an argument with a cowboy. He'd been negligent in watching the gambler deal the hand. Back in Boulder, Sheriff Howell had showed Gideon how a gambler would deal a good hand to a player with a big stake to get them to go all in and then beat them with an even better hand. The deputy suspected he was being set up. He only raised the stakes a dollar on his bet. As the others were discarding, Gideon grinned at his cards and pretended to be too occupied with his hand to notice the dealing. He kept his eyesight just above his cards in order to watch the proceedings. Burton discarded three cards and when he dealt himself the replacements, Gideon spotted him dealing from the bottom of the deck. The gambler was very good at cheating, but not so practiced as not to be spotted.

"You just dealt off the bottom of the deck. I'm guessing you're holding four queens," Gideon accused the gambler as he stood and slammed his palm down upon Burton's cards. He flipped them over, revealing the four queens and a deuce.

"You son of a . . ." Burton said before Gideon leaped across the table and toppled the gambler and his chair to the floor.

Burton let out a loud groan as the deputy's full weight landed upon him. Gideon climbed to a sitting position upon the gambler's stomach and began pummeling him. Jack took a step toward the two men and then stopped. He still suspected that Gideon had gotten what he wanted, but figured if the gambler was foolish enough to cheat Gideon after already having received one whipping – well, he deserved what he got. Gideon didn't stop throwing punches until Burton's face became a bloody mess. He dragged the gambler out of the saloon to a horse trough and threw him into the water. As Gideon held Burton under, the gambler made a desperate attempt to surface. Gideon finally released him before he drowned. Burton shot up out of the water and got to his feet, gasping for air.

"You better be on the first train out of town or I'll give you more of the same. Do you understand me?" Gideon bellowed.

As soon as Burton nodded his head, Gideon unleashed a right hook to the jaw that knocked the gambler out of the trough and onto the ground with a thud. He lay there in an unconscious heap. When Gideon turned to walk back into the saloon, he nearly ran into Jack. The mountain man handed him his hat.

"Are you happy now?" Jack asked.

"What? I don't know what you're talking about. I would have been happy to have kept my winnings instead of scattering them all across the floor," Gideon said as he adjusted his hat to his satisfaction. "But if there's one thing I can't stand, it's a card cheat."

Chapter 17

The day after Gideon's incident with the gambler, Jack strolled into McIntire's General Store for some pipe tobacco. Chloe was busy with a customer so he perused the aisles of goods until she was free.

"I need a plew of Lone Jack," Jack announced.

As Chloe retrieved the tobacco, she said, "Gideon's handling of Burton Rochester is the talk of the town. Most people think that the gambler got what he deserved, but there are a few that thinks Gideon went too far. Since you were with him, I wondered what you thought."

Jack scratched his beard a moment before speaking. "Both camps are probably right. Burton should have been smart enough not to try to cheat Gideon after he'd already gotten a licking the first day we came to town, but Gideon worked him over more than necessary," he said.

Chloe leaned across the counter and lowered her voice even though they were the only two people in the store. "Jack, I need to ask you something. I don't expect you to betray a confidence, but I have to know if you are aware of what happened in Gideon's past that troubles him so."

"You have no idea how hard I've worked to pry that information out of Gideon, but I'm afraid to no avail. He wants to punish himself, and I think he fears telling would lessen his burden. I had hoped that he might confide in you."

"The only thing he ever tells me is that he's not staying in Ellsworth for long. He makes sure I understand that, but not much else. Gideon must have done something really terrible during the war," Chloe said as she handed Jack the tobacco.

"The results might have been terrible, but the intent surely wasn't. On one occasion, he more or less confessed to me that what happened had been an accident," Jack said as he fished his money out of his pocket.

Chloe straightened her posture and pulled her shoulders back. She raised her eyebrows and had a look of indignation. "You mean to tell me he tortures himself and ruins his life over an accident? That's ridiculous."

"Chloe, the Indians say 'Don't judge a man until you walk in his moccasins.' I suggest you take that to heart. I feel pretty certain that Gideon accidently took someone's life. That's a terrible burden to bear – accident or not."

"I suppose you have a point, but it's a crying shame his life is ruined over a misfortune. I'd give anything to help him," Chloe said.

Jack studied Chloe for a moment and concluded that she had already fallen in love with Gideon. He could see it in her eyes, and didn't know what to say to her. A part of him wanted to encourage her in hopes she could be the woman he thought it would take to heal his friend, but the other part of him feared she would only get hurt worse than she probably already was. "I don't know what to tell you. I'm sorry I couldn't be of more help, but I've told you what I know. You'll have to figure the rest out for yourself."

"Thanks for talking with me, Jack. I think I at least understand Gideon a little better. I don't know why things in life always have to be so hard."

"Because it's people's nature to make things hard. You're a fine girl. You make sure you take care of yourself," Jack said and tipped his hat before leaving.

As Jack headed for the hat shop, he saw Burton Rochester carrying his satchel toward the train station. The gambler's face looked so bruised and swollen that he was barely recognizable, and he wore his hat pulled down low in an attempt to conceal the damage. He spotted Jack and made a wide berth around the deputy as he walked toward the depot.

As Jack entered the store, he said, "Your friend the gambler is leaving town."

Gideon looked up from his book with an expression that gave away nothing about his mood. "Good to know. One less scoundrel we have to deal with," he said before returning his gaze to what he was reading.

At breakfast earlier that morning, Jack had noticed an improvement in Gideon's demeanor. The young deputy had at least attempted some small talk and didn't look as if he were miserable. He still wasn't his normal self, but compared to the previous day, he appeared positively joyous.

"I just saw Chloe in the store. You should go see her. I think she's worried about you," Jack said as he began loading his pipe with tobacco.

Glancing up, Gideon gave Jack an annoyed look, but didn't speak. He resumed reading as if nothing had been said.

Sheriff Whitney walked into the shop. "I figured I'd find you boys in here. Are either of you much at tracking?" he asked.

"Jack is as good as they come. He could track an ant across a mountain range," Gideon replied.

Jack managed to grin at the compliment and scowl at Gideon all in the same look.

"Good. Glad to hear that. Hershel Hendricks came to town with his misses for supplies this morning and when they returned home, they'd been robbed. They got some guns and his stash of money. I'd go, but the marshal and I have a meeting with the mayor, and he don't take kindly to me canceling on him. Hershel is at the jail and can take you to his place."

"Somebody must have been watching them or was prepared to rob them at gunpoint if they'd been home," Gideon reasoned.

"I'd say they were being watched. You can see from a long ways around here. Just so you know, Willis Schultz is a neighbor of theirs, but I don't suspect he had a hand in this. He's never done anything like that, but I wanted you to be aware in case you cross paths with him again," the sheriff warned.

"I'm in no mood to tolerate his behavior," Gideon said as he stood and grabbed his hat.

"Just in case the mayor asks the marshal about last night – are you sure you caught Burton Rochester cheating at cards?" Sheriff Whitney asked.

"I saw him deal off the bottom of the deck. He was good at it, but not that good. Sheriff Howell, back in Boulder, taught me how to catch cheats in all the games."

"Let's get to the jail," the sheriff said as he opened the door.

Hershel Hendricks and his wife, Millie, looked to be about fifty. After years of marriage, they had begun to take on each other's facial appearance the way that some couples do. Their skin was weather-beaten and wrinkled from years of working the land. They wore worn, but clean clothes and had an air of respectability about them. Mrs. Hendricks, though clearly traumatized by the robbery, apologized profusely for inconveniencing the law officers.

After Gideon and Jack introduced themselves to the couple, they retrieved their horses from the livery stable and followed the couple's wagon back to their house. Mr. Hendricks showed Gideon the ransacked home. The cupboard, wardrobes, and anything else used for storage had the contents strewn all about the place. Mrs. Hendricks began crying at seeing the mess again.

Jack joined them inside the house a few minutes later. "There are three sets of horse tracks," he said.

"Just out of curiosity, where does Willis Schultz live from here?" Gideon asked.

"He would be the first home you came to if you went straight north of here," Hershel answered.

"You folks try to calm yourself and get your place cleaned up. We'll do our best to try to find your things. What exactly is missing?" Gideon asked.

"They got our thirty-five dollars, a Winchester 1866, and my Parker Brothers shotgun. I still can't believe someone would rob poor folks like us," Hershel replied.

"Some folks would steal the shirt off your back. Try not to worry," Jack said.

"Let's get going," Gideon said as he moved toward the door.

Following the tracks was easy to do in the soft Kansas soil. The robbers had come from the east and returned in the same direction after the robbery. Gideon and Jack followed the tracks to the same creek where Gideon and Chloe had their picnic. The tracks stopped at the water.

"Did they go up or down the creek?" Gideon asked.

Jack squinted his eyes and frowned. "Don't mess with me, son. If you can't tell which direction they went, well then, I didn't teach you nearly as well as I thought I did," he grumbled.

"Looks to me as if they turned their horses north," Gideon said, grinning at the old mountain man. "We're going to end up at Schultz's place, aren't we?"

"I would say so. My guess would be that Willis must have got desperate for some money."

The lawmen followed the creek for about a mile to where the riders had come out of the water and headed back straight west. After a short ride, a house with a barn came into view in the distance. Three horses were turned out in the corral.

"Willis is not only desperate, but stupid, too. A blind man could have followed those tracks," Gideon surmised.

"That might be a good reason for us to use some caution. We know where these tracks are headed and need to move over so we come in behind the barn. Otherwise, we could be target practice," Jack said.

"Old, but wise," Gideon joked.

"But not so old that I couldn't plug you and blame it on Willis."

They moved away from the horse tracks so that the barn blocked their view from the house. Gideon pulled his spyglass from his saddlebag and studied the small ranch. He didn't see a single person moving about the place.

"Maybe they're fixing supper," Gideon said, noting the position of the sun to the west.

"Or waiting until we get in close enough that they can't miss," Jack replied.

"I don't think so. There's not much place to hide and the barn doors are shut."

The lawmen rode right up to the barn and tied their horses. Gideon jogged to the side of the building and peeked around the corner. He still didn't see a sign of a living soul except for smoke pluming from the cook stove chimney.

"Looks like they're cooking their meal," Gideon reported.

"How do you want to handle them?" Jack asked.

"I say we tiptoe up to the house and barge in. Maybe we can catch them with their pants down. I think any other way will be a shootout for sure."

"Let's get going. If I'm going to die, I might as well get it over with."

Gideon and Jack hustled across the yard and stepped lightly onto the porch. As they drew their revolvers, they pulled back the hammers. Jack took a deep breath and nodded his head that he was ready. With a running start, Gideon put his shoulder into the door. The latch gave way with a crack and the two law officers bounded into the room. The two hired hands were sitting at the table, one with his back to Gideon and Jack, and the other facing them. Willis stood at the stove with a spatula in his hand. The surprise of the intrusion had them all looking as if they'd just seen a ghost.

"You're all under arrest for robbery. Don't move," Gideon bellowed.

Willis darted behind the stove, and the man facing the door dove to the floor. The remaining man stood and attempted to draw his gun and spin around to face the lawmen all in one awkward motion. His revolver hadn't cleared the holster before Gideon and Jack both shot him at near point-blank. The force of the blasts hurled the hired hand backwards onto the table and sent it crumbling to the floor.

"Damn it, surrender," Gideon yelled before diving for the floor as Willis pointed his pistol toward him.

Jack ran for the doorway of the adjoining room as Willis swung his arm in that direction and took a shot at the mountain man. A chunk of door frame smacked Jack as he took cover behind the wall.

Gideon found himself no more than ten feet from the remaining ranch hand, lying face to face. The cowboy fired his revolver just before Gideon squeezed off a shot. Searing pain surged through Gideon's chest as he watched the ranch hand jerk from taking a bullet. As the cowboy struggled to take aim again, Gideon began firing. Each shot caused the robber to shudder as he valiantly tried to fire his gun until he collapsed.

Turning his attention to Jack, Gideon saw the mountain man unsuccessfully exchanging shots with Willis. Gideon took a moment to glance at his chest. His shirt was soaked in red. With so much blood, he figured he might be dying. Wishing to help Jack before his strength waned, Gideon scooted across the floor until he could see Willis. The rancher was too occupied with

Jack to notice he had exposed himself to Gideon. With the last live round in his revolver, Gideon took careful aim at Willis's head and fired. Willis collapsed as if he'd been dropped from the gallows, dead before he hit the ground.

Jack saw Willis go down and then looked toward Gideon. Blood seemed to be the only thing that he could see, and he came barreling toward his friend. "I'm coming," he yelled.

"I think it might be bad. My chest is burning like it's on fire," Gideon moaned.

When Jack kneeled down, he grabbed Gideon's shirt and ripped it open. There was too much blood to see the wound. He jumped up and found a towel that look fairly clean. After rushing back to Gideon, Jack soaked up the blood a couple of times before realizing what he was seeing. He applied the towel one more time before touching Gideon's chest with his fingers.

Gideon raised his head up off the floor. "Well, damn it, say something. How bad is it?" he asked.

Jack dropped to his butt and let out a loud sigh. "You scared the hell out of me. You have a chest full of wood shards. I don't think any of them penetrated your chest wall. They look to be under the skin and through your chest muscles, but there are some big ones."

Gideon laughed with relief in spite of the considerable pain. "I thought I was dying. It hurts like hell. Get them out of me."

"I don't have anything but a knife and I ain't about to try that. You'll have to wait until we get you to a doctor."

Gideon sat up and pointed to a hole in the floor. "I guess I'm wearing the wood that used to go right there."

"That's a heap better than wearing lead. We had better leave all this and get you into town. The sheriff and marshal can worry about the bodies. That wood will likely cause festering," Jack said.

"Jack, you're a good friend."

"Don't be getting all sappy with me just because you thought you were going to die," Jack said as he got to his feet and held out his hand to pull Gideon up to his feet.

Chapter 18

Gideon and Jack walked into the doctor's office just as the physician was readying to leave for the day. Dr. Horatio Bell all but grinned at the sight of so much dried blood on Gideon's shirt and chest. The doctor loved to work on wounds and considered them his specialty.

Dr. Bell had a reputation for being a fine physician. He personally would have even gone so far as to consider his skills as exceptional. Unfortunately, his high opinion of himself had led to his dismissal from several hospitals back east and garnered him a reputation that had eventually made it necessary to move farther west. Hence, he now lived in what he considered the godforsaken town of Ellsworth with his nagging wife who possibly hated the place even more than he did.

The doctor looked to be in his mid-forties with a small potbelly that he tended to rub when concentrating. He overcompensated for his receding hairline with bushy mutton chop sideburns that were connected by way of his massive mustache.

After Dr. Bell had Gideon remove his shirt, the doctor led his new patient to a table and asked, "What do we have here?"

"A bullet drove wood splinters from the floor into my chest," Gideon answered.

"So, no bullet wound then?"

"I don't think so."

Gideon noticed that the news seemed to take some of the enthusiasm out of Dr. Bell. Seeing the doctor's reaction griped Gideon to no end. He'd had his share of physicians with high opinions of themselves before and had had about all of them that he ever cared to encounter. If he hadn't needed someone that knew what they were doing to remove the wood pieces, Gideon would have marched out of the office.

The doctor heated some water, and when it was hot, dunked a towel into it. He then placed the cloth on Gideon's chest to soften the blood. After the blood moistened, the doctor began scrubbing the mess away, causing Gideon considerable pain.

"Sorry to do this, but I have to get your chest clean," Dr. Bell said when Gideon winced.

"I bet you wish I was shot so you could treat that instead of splinters," Gideon said testily.

"While that would certainly be more interesting, I do not wish injury to anyone. I've heard of your reputation around town. Maybe we are alike in that we both like a good challenge."

Jack had to cover his mouth with his hand to keep from making a grin. Gideon spotted him anyway and cut his eyes.

"Do you want me to put you to sleep? I'm going to have to make some cuts to get some of the wood out. It will hurt like all get out," Dr. Bell said.

"No, I'd rather have the pain than go through that. Just get it over with," Gideon said.

The doctor had to use a scalpel to open a couple of the wounds enough to get the shards removed. Gideon hollered in pain once when the doctor used forceps to pull the wood out of his chest muscle. In all, the doctor removed five shards of wood ranging in length from one to five inches. He also had to pick out numerous small splinters. When he dropped the last one onto the tray, he said, "You're not the first patient that I've had to remove splinters from that was the result of a gunshot, but you certainly are the worst case I've ever treated. You are going to be sore. And God knows what might have been on that floorboard. You will more than likely get some festering."

"I lived through a war and I'll surely live through this," Gideon remarked.

Dr. Bell retrieved a bottle of iodine and covered Gideon's chest with the medicine. "You will need to wash your chest twice a day with soap and then reapply the iodine. I'm not going to put any stitches in you. I'd rather keep the wounds free to drain." He then grabbed a tincture of willow bark and handed the vial to the deputy. "Take a spoonful of this if the pain gets too bad."

"Thank you, doctor."

The doctor turned toward Jack. "To be honest, I don't really trust this patient's judgement in whether he will need further treatment. If he gets to feeling ill, I'm counting on you to either come get me or drag his ass in here."

Jack winked at the doctor. "That you can count on. And you pegged him just about right. He's got a head as hard as an anvil and suspect judgement coming from it."

Gideon paid the doctor two dollars for his services, and left the office bare-chested. He and Jack walked back to the house, finding George cooking supper. The hatmaker could barely contain himself to finish fixing the meal after seeing Gideon's wounds. When they all sat down to eat, George begged Gideon and Jack to recount the day's happenings. His eyes grew big with astonishment, and he stopped eating to listen. He kept interrupting the men with questions until he knew every detail of the shootout.

"You two sure live a lot more exciting life than me making hats," George remarked.

"But there's a whole lot less pain involved," Gideon noted.

After the meal, Gideon strapped on his gun belt.

"Where do you think you're going?" Jack asked.

"Don't play momma with me. My chest barely hurts right now and I feel fine. We need to tell the sheriff what happened together anyway. I'll work tonight in case I'm not up for it in a day or two," Gideon said in his typical dry manner.

Jack shook his head in disgust. "I know there's no point in arguing with you. It would be a waste of my breath. But I jest you not, if you get sick, I'll lay you out and carry you on my back to the doctor if I have to."

"Duly noted."

Sheriff Whitney and Marshal Morco were both impressed with Gideon and Jack's prowess in the shootout. They were as awed by the event as George had been and asked many of the same questions. Marshal Morco even requested that Gideon show off his wounds.

With the day already getting late, the sheriff decided to wait until the following day to retrieve the bodies. The next morning the sheriff and marshal recovered the two stolen guns and found the money stuffed in Willis's pocket.

∞

By Sunday, Gideon was running a fever and the wounds were oozing pus. When he came into the kitchen for breakfast, Jack immediately noticed that Gideon's eyes looked dull and his coloring was sallow. Jack coaxed Gideon into drinking some water and eating some eggs, but he went back to bed as soon as he finished his meal. When Jack came into the bedroom to say that he was going for the doctor, Gideon nodded his head without an argument.

Dr. Bell didn't appreciate being summoned on a Sunday morning while reading his newspaper and sipping coffee. He walked into George's house all in a huff and marched into the bedroom without saying a word.

"Why didn't you come see me yesterday?" Dr. Bell griped.

"Because I felt fine yesterday. I woke up this way," Gideon answered.

"Well, let's see it."

Gideon unbuttoned his shirt and opened it. The doctor bent over and peered at the wounds. He took his finger and pressed against one of the punctures, causing Gideon to wince and pus to shoot out of the wound.

"Get me some warm water and soap," the doctor barked.

By the time that Jack carried the soap and water into the room, Dr. Bell, much to Gideon's relief, had finished draining all of the wounds. The doctor scrubbed Gideon's chest and reapplied a coating of iodine.

"Have you been taking the willow bark tincture?" Dr. Bell asked.

"I wasn't in any pain until you started mashing around on me," Gideon replied.

"Take a spoonful every four hours. It will bring down your fever. You need plenty of liquids."

Jack took a step forward. "Chloe is bringing some soup over later. That should be good for you."

"Yes, it will," the doctor agreed.

In an exasperated tone, Gideon asked, "How did Chloe know anything about this?"

"I might have seen her on the way to getting the doctor," Jack replied.

"Might have? Was she just roaming the streets on a Sunday morning?"

"I stopped by her house for a moment."

"You old goat. One of these days you'll be sitting around making quilts with all the old ladies and gossiping up a storm."

The doctor shut his bag. "I have better things to do than listen to this bickering. I'll come by in the morning."

"How sick is he?" Jack asked.

"He's not well, but he's young and strong. As long as he takes care of himself, I expect he will be just fine. If he ignores his condition, he could die," Dr. Bell said.

"Oh, he's going to take care of himself – that I can grant you. Even if I have to tie him to the bed," Jack said.

"Very well. See you tomorrow." The doctor showed himself out the door.

"I'm not happy with you," Gideon said.

"Well, that's more the norm than the exception these days. Chloe cares about you and I thought she should know. She's the one that insisted on bringing the soup over to you. Once she gets here, George and I are going fishing," Jack stated.

Gideon bolted up in bed. "What? You're just setting Chloe up for disappointment. She and I came to an understanding and you are going to get in the middle of it."

"George and I had already planned on going fishing. Everything is not about you."

"Why didn't you invite me then?"

"Same reason you didn't invite me on your horse ride. Sometimes three's a crowd."

As Gideon dropped back into the bed, he closed his eyes and said nothing further, prompting Jack to leave the room.

Chloe arrived just before noon carrying a big pot of chicken and noodle soup. George led her into the kitchen while Jack summoned Gideon. While George sliced a loaf of bread, Chloe filled four bowls with soup.

"How are you feeling?" Chloe asked as Gideon entered the kitchen.

Gideon moved slowly and sat down gingerly, grimacing from the soreness. "I'm not feeling that ill. Mother Jack likes to lord over his chicks," Gideon replied.

"The doctor said he could die if he's not careful," Jack interjected.

"Eat some soup. My momma always said it was good for what ails you," Chloe said.

As the group was eating, Jack offhandedly said, "George and I are going fishing. Chloe, you're welcome to stay as long as you like. I'm not sure our patient can be trusted to be left to his own devices."

"You and George go have a good time. I don't mind babysitting at all," Chloe said, causing the brothers to burst into laughter.

Gideon tried to grin good-naturedly, but the tight way he held his mouth gave away the embarrassment Chloe's remark caused him.

After finishing the soup, Jack and George made a hasty exit of the home, leaving the dirty dishes. Chloe took it upon herself to clean up the mess.

As Chloe heated water, she asked, "Do you need to lie down?"

"I'll need to take a nap here shortly, but I'll sit up until you're finished with what you're doing," Gideon replied.

"Sounds like you came close to getting yourself killed."

"Closer than I like – that's for sure. Jack and I might have misjudged how easily we could apprehend Willis and his men."

"So it wasn't a death wish then?"

The question caused Gideon to rub his scar. "No. I thought I had taken a bullet to the chest and was dying. I assure you that that notion didn't bring me any satisfaction."

"I didn't mean to upset you, but I was curious," Chloe said as she poured the heated water into a tub.

"Chloe, I know you must think I'm crazy. And truth be told, there are times I wonder if life is worth living, but I've never tried to get myself killed."

"I wish I could fix you," Chloe said as she plopped the bowls into the water.

"Well, you can't, so quit worrying about it."

"If the terrible thing that you did in your past was an accident, does it really make sense to punish yourself? Wouldn't making the most of your life to atone for your mistake accomplish more?"

"Who said it was an accident?" Gideon asked suspiciously.

"That's the impression that I got."

"No, that's the information that you got from talking to Jack behind my back."

"What if I did? Is it so wrong for me to care? If you are going to be a damn fool about your life, somebody needs to look out for you. I've never known a man with so much potential for good to be so hell-bent on ruining his life."

Gideon got to his feet. "I need to go rest," he said before walking out the room.

∞

The Dolan brothers had been fishing in the Smoky Hill River for over an hour with the only thing to show for their effort being a bruise on George's shoulders from not being warned of the penchant for biting of Gideon's horse.

"I thought you said this was a good spot," Jack complained.

"It usually is. Maybe you're just bad luck. Just enjoy the day and quit being so crotchety," George retorted.

"That darn fool Gideon has me worried."

"He's doing what the doctor asked of him. What more can he do?"

"Nothing, I suppose. I didn't tell Gideon this, but I used to know this mountain man named Skunk Harris. Even when he was a young man, he had a streak of white hair down the middle of his head. Anyway, we used to trap together some. Skunk got a splinter in his finger and he wouldn't let me get it out. He wouldn't mess with it either. Said it would work its way out on its own. So it gets to festering and he still won't touch it. His finger began turning black and then his hand. When it started traveling up his arm, he was so sick he couldn't move. I had to cut off his arm, but he died anyway. I buried him best I could up in the mountains. I guess that experience made me gun-shy about splinters and such."

"Gideon is under doctor's care, and Dr. Bell is a good one even if he isn't the friendliest fellow you've ever met," George said.

"I suppose so."

"Since we're on the subject of mountain men, how did the son of a hatmaker ever end up in that solitary life? I always hoped you'd go into the family business with me, but you left home, and the next thing I know, you're writing the folks saying you're in the mountains learning how to trap."

Jack set the fishing pole down and pulled his pipe from his pocket. He carefully packed the bowl with Lone Jack before striking a match and puffing until the tobacco burned to his satisfaction. "The truth of the matter is that I just prefer my own company most of the time. I guess that's why you probably thought I never cared a lick for you, and it's why I always hated school. I like being alone. Don't get me wrong, I've enjoyed our time together here in Ellsworth, and I think I've helped keep Gideon out of too much trouble, but to be honest, I'm ready to get home and get my traps oiled up for the coming season. I'm looking forward to cold weather. George, there is nothing more peaceful than being up in the mountains when it is bitter cold and snow is coming down the size of silver dollars. It's like I can feel God in every flake."

George was gazing at his brother with wonderment when his line went taut. He pulled in a nice channel catfish. The mood was broken, but the fish started biting.

∞

After Chloe had finished cleaning the kitchen, she walked into the bedroom to find Gideon sleeping. She sat down in a chair and watched him. His breathing sounded easy and rhythmic, and he looked at peace. She already regretted her actions earlier in the kitchen. Sometimes her heart got in the way of her mouth. She knew she was fighting a losing battle and needed to accept surrender. Realizing that this would probably be the only time she ever got to watch the man she loved sleep, she contented herself with enjoying the opportunity she had with him.

When Gideon opened his eyes a couple of hours later, he startled at seeing Chloe watching him.

"Hello," he said sheepishly.

"Hello, yourself."

"I'm sorry I snapped at you earlier."

"I had it coming. I'm the one that's sorry. I should have minded my own business," Chloe said.

"Nothing wrong with being a caring person. It just gets you into trouble once in a while and it probably never gets you the appreciation that you deserve," Gideon said as he sat up in bed.

"So, Gideon, are we still friends?"

"Always, Chloe."

Chapter 19

True to his word, Dr. Bell arrived early Monday morning at George's house. Having just finished their breakfasts, the men were still sitting at the table, sipping coffee and talking. The doctor rushed Gideon to the bedroom and did a quick exam, once again pressing on the wounds to drain away pus. He seemed pleased with Gideon's improvement, ordering him to another day of rest with instructions to come by the office on Tuesday afternoon.

Gideon spent the day resting and was glad when Chloe stopped by to check on him after work. If she felt any awkwardness from the quarrel on Sunday, she didn't show it. Once she felt satisfied that Gideon's health was improving, she headed home.

By noon on Tuesday, Gideon felt well enough to be about stir-crazy from being trapped in the house. He heated water and managed to relax as he soaked in the tub. After scrubbing and a shave, he put on clean clothes and headed for the doctor's office.

"I can just look at you and see that you are much improved," Dr. Bell said upon seeing his patient walk through the door.

"I feel fine. Anything has to be better for me than another day of sitting in that house," Gideon replied.

The examination revealed that the wounds had stopped festering and were beginning to scab over. Gideon's temperature had also returned to normal.

"You can go back to work as long as you promise to keep your wounds clean. Also, keep applying the iodine until the scabs are completely formed. You don't need to be getting into any brawls and crawling around on those wretched saloon floors either," the doctor warned.

"I will do everything you say – I promise. I don't want to relapse. I'm too stiff and sore to get into a scrape anyway. Thank you for taking care of me," Gideon said.

"We all have our jobs to do. If you need my services again, try to make it something interesting like a bullet wound," Dr. Bell said in an attempt at a little macabre humor.

"Will do," Gideon said as he eased off the table.

Gideon felt so good at being out of the house that his step had a bit of a bounce to it as he walked to the hat shop. "I hoped you boys might be off fishing again. I sure wouldn't mind another batch of those catfish. They certainly were tasty."

As George studied a hat to make sure he had the same roll of the brim on both sides, he said, "When you are well, you and Jack should grab the poles and go some morning."

"The doctor said I could go back to work. I might need to wait a few more days before I play in the mud."

During Gideon and George's conversation, Jack had remained hidden behind a newspaper. He lowered it enough to peek over the top. "Just because you can work, it don't mean you can act like a heathen. You need to keep those wounds clean," he said.

"Yes, Jack. That's why I said I would wait to go fishing. You really are overdoing this mother hen business," Gideon said.

Satisfied with the hat, George set it down and said, "He saw a man die from a splinter. He's got a real phobia from that experience."

Jack shot George a look that might have put the fear of death into anybody but his brother. "You never could keep a secret."

Gideon opened his mouth to tease Jack and then stopped short. He had a sudden epiphany that everybody had something from their past that they carried around with them like a ball and chain – even the self-reliant Jack Dolan. "Well, I'm just glad that Jack was there to help take care of me."

Expecting to be hounded unmercifully, the compliment so took Jack by surprise that he looked taken aback. He decided to change the subject and said, "Word is that another couple of herds arrived late yesterday and more are expected in today. The town should be wild tonight."

"I guess we won't have to worry about being bored then," Gideon said.

∞

Ellsworth turned into a booming town that week as the cattle herds arrived one after another. The merchants were giddy from all the business. The hat shop had such a run on merchandise that George had to work extra hours to keep up with demand. Jack helped him whenever time allowed. Chloe had stocked up on plenty of supplies for the expected onslaught of business and had managed to keep the shelves full, but when Gideon paid the store a visit, Sean and his daughter both looked exhausted from all the hustle-bustle.

The news of the lynching of the cowboy had spread from trail crew to trail crew like a prairie fire. While the actions of the vigilantes didn't turn the cowboys into angels, it did put a stop to the crews racing into town and firing their weapons. Most nights, Gideon and Jack spent their time breaking up fights between the different crews and settling disputes between cowboys and whores over payments for services rendered. When they encountered a cowboy that acted too mad or drunk to reason with, they'd throw him in jail until morning and then send him on his way with a warning.

Cattle buyers had arrived by train and liked to make their way around town flashing their wads of cash and wearing nice suits. Once they had checked into the hotel, they would make a beeline to the bank and set up an account to deposit most of the money they brought with them. At night, they would hold high stakes games of poker amongst themselves in back rooms of the saloons, tipping the saloon girls generously to keep their whiskey glasses filled and their cigars lit.

Whenever Gideon got the chance to talk to a trail boss, he would inquire about the possibility of joining up with the crew for the return trip. Most had been receptive to hiring him with the condition that he would have to pay his own expenses back to the ranch. The problem was that none of the bosses struck Gideon as somebody he would really want to be his boss. Most of them had personalities as dry as a desert and a couple of the bosses gave Gideon the impression that they were just plain mean. He feared he'd end up doing something he'd regret if one of them unleashed his wrath upon him or another crewmember. He also had second thoughts about returning to being a ranch hand. At times in the past, he'd enjoyed the solitude of the work and he knew he would seek the quiet life again, but as of now, he felt content being a deputy in Ellsworth. He hadn't had any trouble sleeping since being injured and liked the idea of staying put until his past would force him to run again.

Friday night turned out to be a busy one. Not only had all the cowboys come to town, but a good many of the townsfolk were in the saloons, too. Gideon and Jack had already arrested two men, and deputies Webb Schafer and Mort Hall had arrested one cowboy.

Word traveled into the Cowboy Palace that things were getting wild down the street in the Rusty Nail. All of the deputies headed toward the seediest saloon in town. A gunshot rang out from inside just as Gideon and Jack hit the door. The building was so full of tobacco and gun smoke that it was hard to breathe. In the dim light, a cowboy could be seen dancing on a table with his revolver in the air while the piano player pounded on the keys for all he was worth. Deputy Schafer was futilely trying to talk the cowboy to put his gun away and come down from the table.

Gideon maneuvered to the piano and yanked the fallboard down over the keys, pinching the piano player's fingers in the process. The sudden stop in the music caused all eyes to turn that way.

"You need to put that gun away and get down – right now," Gideon yelled.

The cowboy scowled at the deputy. "I'm just having fun and ain't hurting nobody."

"The whores upstairs might think differently if you shoot one of them," Gideon said.

"You lawmen all think you own the world. You can go to . . ."

Jack snuck up from behind and gave the table a hard shove with his foot. The cowboy looked as if he were trying to dance in air as he valiantly attempted to keep his balance. He crashed to the floor headfirst. Before he could even moan, Jack snatched the cowboy's gun from his hand.

"That was quick work for an old man," Gideon said as he joined Jack.

"Yeah, I didn't want my sensitive ears to have to endure a gunshot when he plugged you," Jack said.

Gideon turned toward Deputy Schafer. "We'll drag him to jail and head back to the Cowboy Palace if you boys can keep an eye on this place."

"That'll work," Deputy Schafer responded.

After locking up the cowboy, Gideon and Jack stayed in the Cowboy Palace until it emptied of patrons. Preston Edwards, the saloon owner, grabbed a bottle of his best whiskey and poured two glasses.

"You boys earned a reward tonight," Preston said before walking away and grabbing a broom.

Jack took his first sip. "Now that's some good whiskey – smooth," he said.

After taking a drink, Gideon concurred. "You have to admit that this is a lot better than freezing your ass off on some mountain skinning beaver."

With a chuckle, Jack said, "I always have a bottle of good whiskey with me on the mountain, and I've never had a beaver try to shoot me yet."

Chapter 20

With the trail crews and cattle buyers all flooded into Ellsworth, Saturday had been a hectic day at the bank. Phillip Tyrone gladly ushered out the last customer of the day and locked the door to the business. On his walk home, he had Lisa Young on his mind. She had come in earlier that day to make a money withdrawal and had slipped him a note requesting he pay her a visit if at all possible that night. Just the touch of Lisa's hand had aroused him when he had taken the note from her. Phillip figured he must be Lisa's only suitor now that Lonnie Wilson remained locked up in the jail awaiting trial for murder. His mind raced for an excuse to give to his wife so that he could leave the house that evening. He contemplated telling her that the cattle buyers had invited him to a gathering and that he really needed to go for the sake of bank business. At times like this he wondered why he bothered deceiving his wife instead of just coming out and telling her how things were going to be from now on. He hated her, and had only married the frigid battle-ax because her daddy was rich and had gotten him started in the banking business.

Phillip entered his home and was surprised not to be greeted by his wife. She usually made the pretense of acting as if they were a happy couple and would have a drink waiting in hand for him.

"Faye," Phillip called out.

He strolled into the kitchen and was startled so badly that he squealed and made a little bunny hop as he threw his hands into the air at finding his wife gagged and bound to a chair. Two men with masks and their hats pulled low were pointing revolvers at him. Phillip thought he would die on the spot from his heart exploding in his chest. He grabbed a chair for support as he became dizzy.

"If you want you and your wife to live, you'll do everything we say," the shorter of the two men said and cocked his gun for emphasis.

"What do you want?" Phillip asked.

"Sit down."

The other masked man tied Phillip to a chair.

"After it gets dark, you are going to take us to the bank and open the vault. We have no desire to do you or your wife harm as long as you follow orders."

"You don't want to do this. The law will track you down," Phillip warned.

"Listen to you sitting here in your fancy house. The only difference between you and me is that banks get to rob people legally.

"I'm just the vice president. Only the bank president has the combination," Phillip pleaded.

The shorter man looked at his partner. "I guess we made a mistake. Go ahead and kill them then."

"Wait. Wait. Wait. I'll open the vault," Phillip cried out.

"You aren't listening very well. That's one mark against you already. Do not lie to me again. If you do, I'll cut off one of your fingers."

The color drained from Phillip's face. He looked over at his wife and actually felt a smidgen of compassion for her. Her eyes were wild with fear and she looked ready to burst into tears at any moment.

"Gag him, too. We're going to be here awhile."

The taller of the intruders lit wood in the cooking stove and began peeling potatoes. He tossed them into a pot of water on the stove and then placed the steaks that Faye had planned to fix for dinner that night into a skillet. He tapped his toe and hummed "Dixie" as he prepared the meal. When the food was cooked, the men carried their plates to the parlor so they could pull down their masks to eat. After they finished eating, they returned to the kitchen to sit and wait as the hours passed while the big one tapped his fingernails on the wood table.

When the clock on the mantel chimed the twelve times for midnight, the men untied Phillip.

"We're going to walk to the bank now. You will die if you try anything and so will your wife. Do I make myself clear?" the shorter one asked.

"I'm not about to get myself killed over the bank's money. Are you really going to let us live?" Phillip asked.

"That's the plan if you do as you are told. We aren't in the habit of killing just for sport."

After grabbing their saddlebags and rope, the men exited the house out the back door and followed the alley toward the bank. The thieves made sure to avoid the light of the streetlamps as they made their way. Phillip felt so weak and faint that only his fear of death gave him the determination to walk. Once they arrived at the side of the bank, the men watched the street from the shadows. A good number of the cowboys had returned to the herds by then, but a few stragglers were milling in front of the saloons.

Once the street finally cleared of people, the shorter man stuck his revolver in Phillip's back and said, "Get your key out and let's go."

Phillip trembled so badly that he had to hold his keys with both hands to unlock the door. As soon as he opened it, the robbers shoved him into the bank. One of them struck a match and pushed Phillip behind the counter. The taller one put an oil lamp on the floor and lit the wick.

"Go get it open and we'll be gone."

After Phillip failed to open the vault on his first two attempts, he heard one of the men cock his gun.

"I'll get it open. Just be patient. I've never been robbed before," Phillip pleaded.

His succeeded in entering the combination correctly on his next try. One of the men shoved the banker to the floor to make his way to the money in the vault. As the outlaws filled their saddlebags, they laughed and joked on the ease of their heist.

Once the vault was emptied, the shorter man said, "Sit down in that chair."

Phillip did as instructed, silently praying that his life was not about to end. The men bound him so securely that he couldn't even move his legs. They then gagged him.

"Thank you for your cooperation. It has been our pleasure doing business with your fine bank. You have a nice evening," the taller of the men said before blowing out the lamp. The men scrambled out of the building and disappeared into the night.

∞

Phillip and Faye Tyrone were prominent members of the Lutheran Church and attended service weekly. The banker's reason for being a member of the congregation was purely career serving. He got the opportunity to make a good name for himself with his willingness to always help in church functions and to hobnob with some of Ellsworth's wealthiest families.

Some of Faye's friends were particularly troubled by her absence from service. If Faye was in town, she just didn't miss coming to church. The women feared that Phillip and Faye had come down with something and were too ill to get out of the house. They talked amongst themselves and decided to go check on the couple. When no one answered the door at the Tyrone residence, Martha Hayes stuck her head inside and called out. After hearing no response, the women cautiously entered the home together. All three of them screamed in unison when they stepped into the kitchen and saw Faye tied to the chair. Faye looked horrible. Her eyes were puffy and desperate with fear, and the room reeked of urine. The women, overcoming their thoughts of fleeing, scrambled to free Faye from her bindings and help her to her feet.

"My God, Faye, what happened?"

Faye's mouth and throat were so parched that she could only say, "Drink."

She gulped down two glasses of water before recounting in bits and pieces all that had happened the previous night.

Martha assumed herself the natural leader of the group and took charge. "I'm going to go get the marshal. You two help Faye get herself cleaned up before we get back," she ordered.

Faye held out her hand to slow her friend's departure. "First have the marshal go to the bank to check on Phillip. I pray those men let him live."

Martha tracked down the sheriff and marshal having lunch in the café. She came to their table talking so excitedly that the marshal had to make her sit down and take a breath before starting over. By the time she finished delivering her news, the whole café buzzed in a panic over their bank accounts.

The sheriff and marshal ran to the bank and found the door unlocked. They hurried inside with their weapons drawn. When they found Phillip all alone, they bolted the door and hurried over to assist him.

Sheriff Whitney looked into the emptied vault and said, "This is liable to cost me an election."

Marshal Morco gave the sheriff a disgusted look before turning his attention to Phillip. "Did you recognize the men?"

Phillip rubbed his wrist trying to get some circulation going in his hand. "I have never seen them before yesterday. They wore masks. About all I can tell you is that one of them is over six feet tall and the leader is maybe five feet eight and stocky. They were waiting at the house so they had to be watching me before yesterday,"

Marshal Morco turned toward the sheriff. "Why don't you go round up Gideon and Jack? They've already proved their merit when they bucked up against Willis Schultz and his men. I'll walk with Phillip to his house. We'll meet back at the jail."

When the three men stepped outside, they were greeted by a throng of townsfolk anxious to see if their savings were all gone.

The sheriff held his hands up to quiet the crowd. "Folks, the bank has been robbed. We will do everything we can to get your money back. If any of you saw a couple of men, one tall and the other shorter and thickset, loitering around the bank the last couple of days, wait for me at the jail. Now let us do our jobs."

By the time the sheriff returned to the jail with Gideon and Jack, the marshal had made his way back from the Tyrone home. Two of the town's residents were waiting for the law officers. Both witnesses had similar descriptions of two men they had noticed that didn't strike them as the usual cowboys from the herds. The tall robber was described as being in his early thirties with dark hair and wearing a black coat even in the heat of the day. The other man looked a little older with light brown hair and a scar running across his chin. They were seen riding a buckskin and a chestnut.

"At least we have somewhat of an idea what they look like," the marshal said after the witnesses had been ushered out of the jail.

"But no idea of which direction they went. We need to try to find their tracks before everybody coming and going into town covers them up," Sheriff Whitney said.

"So how are we going to handle this?" Marshal Morco asked.

"I figure I can lay in some supplies while Jack and Gideon try to find the horse tracks. Then I'll go with them to find the robbers. You can hold down things in town. We need somebody here to keep the cowboys in line and to calm the townsfolk. Them and the cattle buyers are going to be riled up good worrying about their money," the sheriff said.

"The vigilantes are liable to hang me next while you're gone," Marshal Morco lamented. "Let's get to it."

Gideon and Jack retrieved their horses from the livery stable and rode to the edge of Ellsworth. They split up and each made a semicircle around the town, meeting back up on the opposite side.

"Did you find anything?" Jack asked.

"I found some tracks of two horses going northeast in a lope," Gideon replied.

"I'd say you found the right ones then. I didn't find nothing."

"Time's a wasting. Let's go tell the sheriff."

After reporting in at the jail, Gideon and Jack made a quick stop at George's house to get their slickers and a change of clothes. The trio of lawmen then left Ellsworth on the road going northeast.

"Do you think those are the right tracks?" Gideon asked Jack once they were far enough away from town to distinguish the hoof prints that Gideon thought were those of the robbers.

"I do. Whoever made those tracks were in a hurry to get out of town and they're in the wrong direction to be the trail crews," Jack surmised.

"They have a half day lead on us."

Sheriff Whitney looked over at the deputies. "I've been pondering on that. I'm thinking they figured it would be Monday before anybody realized the bank had been robbed. Maybe they won't be pushing their horses too hard and we can catch them before they're halfway across the country."

Jack tugged on his beard, trying to decide whether to hold his tongue. "I think that is just plain foolish thinking. If I made the haul that those boys just did, I'd be lighting a fire under my horse's tail."

"I haven't encountered many mountain men such as yourself, but everyone that I have met is as full of opinions as a goose is full of shit," the sheriff said before spurring his horse into a lope.

Chapter 21

The lawmen had followed the trail of the robbers for only a couple of miles when the horse tracks changed from those made at a lope to ones left at a trot.

Sheriff Whitney, once a scout for the army, called out, "There wasn't much moonlight yesterday. Looks like our robbers were afeared to push their horses in the dark of night."

"We should make up some ground on them," Gideon replied.

After a couple hours of riding, the law officers came upon the spot where the robbers had made camp. They stopped and watered the horses at the creek there while they looked around the campsite.

"How far do you figure we've rode?" Gideon asked.

"This here creek is supposed to be about fourteen miles from town," Sheriff Whitney said.

"Looks like our outlaws weren't too worried about covering much ground before bedding down for the night," Gideon said.

"That gets back to my point that they didn't think they'd be found out until Monday," the sheriff said as he gave Jack a look that dared the mountain man to contest his comment.

"Well, they'll probably be correct in their assessment if we stand around here all day talking," Jack said before walking toward the horses.

Sheriff Whitney made sure he demonstrated that he remained in charge by setting the pace of the journey. The land was flat and the road well kept, making travel easy on the horses. He'd alternate his gelding's gait between a lope and a fast trot while occasionally slowing to a walk to let the animals rest.

About an hour after stopping at the campsite, Jack suddenly held up his hand and yelled, "Whoa." He jumped from his horse and picked up a horseshoe. As he looked about, he bent down and picked something else up off the ground. "The horse's rear foot caught the horseshoe on his front foot and pulled off the shoe. It tore out a junk of hoof wall."

"That should slow them down," the sheriff said.

"Where can they get a fresh horse?" Gideon asked.

"Unless they steal one, Salina is the next town big enough to have a livery stable," Sheriff Whitney replied.

With the realization that the outlaws would be slowed, the lawmen resumed their pursuit at a brisk pace. The hoof prints soon made it apparent that the horse that threw a shoe was going lame. Even then, the tracks proved that the robbers bypassed a couple of small settlements without stopping to try to find another horse.

At sunset, the sheriff, Gideon, and Jack rode into Salina, Kansas. Sheriff Whitney knew the town marshal and stopped in front of the jail. No one was inside besides a couple of prisoners, so the sheriff headed for the lawman's favorite saloon. He spotted the marshal standing at the bar, laughing with a couple of men.

"Walt, how the hell are you?" Sheriff Whitney bellowed.

The marshal looked up in surprise at hearing his name called and then grinned. "Chauncey, what brings you to town?" he asked.

"A couple of men robbed our bank and I believe they came through Salina today. I wonder if you saw them."

"Nah, but I don't see every single rider that passes this way."

"This here is Gideon and Jack. They're a couple of fine deputies," Sheriff Whitney proclaimed.

The marshal pumped each man's hand. "I'm Walt Leinberger. Glad to meet you fellows."

Gideon took an immediate liking to Marshal Leinberger. The marshal had a friendly face with a bushy mustache that he waxed into handlebars, and lively little eyes that twinkled with merriment.

Sheriff Whitney cleared his throat to bring attention back to himself. "I'm thinking they probably stopped at the livery stable. They have a lame horse."

"Well, by golly, let's go have a chat with Scotty," the marshal said before guzzling down the rest of his beer.

The livery stable sat on the opposite side of town from which the lawmen had come. The four men walked toward it while the sheriff and marshal caught up on each other's lives.

"Scotty, are you in there?" the marshal hollered.

The blacksmith stepped out of the room where he lived at the stable. Like most in his trade, he had massive arms and shoulders. His short height and wide girth made him look like a human cannonball. Scotty smiled at the marshal. "Hey, Walt, what can I do for you?"

"Did you have a couple of riders stop in today – one of them on a lame horse?" Walt asked.

"I sure did."

Sheriff Whitney took a step forward to learn more. "What time was that?" he asked in his impatience.

"Best I recollect, it was right around three in the afternoon."

"Those men robbed a bank in Ellsworth. Did you do business with them?" the sheriff asked.

"I thought that the shorter one seemed awfully nervous about something. He couldn't stand still. I took in both of their horses in a trade for a bay and a dun of mine. They didn't even dicker on the price – just handed me the money and were on their way," Scotty said.

The sheriff sighed. "Did the short one have a scar across his chin?"

"He sure did. I remember that he signed the bill of sale as Tom Jackson."

"I doubt that's his real name, but at least we know we're after the right men," the sheriff said.

"As I led out their new horses, I overheard them arguing. The one that signed his name Tom said that they needed to make it on into Junction City because they'd lost too much time," Scotty said.

Marshal Leinberger patted the blacksmith on the back. "Thank you, Scotty. That's good information. You come by the saloon later and I'll buy you a beer."

"What now?" Gideon asked.

In the growing darkness, the sheriff seemed hesitant to answer. He looked over at Scotty. "Do you have three good horses that we can rent?"

"Sure do and the marshal can vouch for me that I'll treat your horses proper whilst you're gone," Scotty replied.

Jack let out a groan and mumbled under his breath.

The sheriff turned toward Gideon and Jack. "I know you boys don't want to hear this, but here's what I think. I need to send a telegram to the sheriff in Junction City to tell him to be on the lookout for our men. We then need to get us a good hot meal. And unfortunately, I believe we need to ride on into Junction City. It will be about morning when we get to town, but if our thieves aren't already in jail, we'll at least be right there with them. Otherwise, I fear we're liable to be chasing them all the way to St. Louie."

Gideon rubbed his scar and grunted. "As much as it pains me to say it, I think you are right."

Jack groaned again. "My fart hole will never be the same."

Marshal Leinberger got to laughing so hard that he got choked, and the sheriff had to beat on the marshal's back while giggling himself. Gideon was so used to such comments that he just shook his head and grinned.

Once the marshal got his breath, he said, "Scotty, make sure you rent these men your best horses."

After Sheriff Whitney sent a telegram to the sheriff in Junction City, Marshal Leinberger joined the others for dinner at his favorite café. The sheriff and marshal had known each other since their days together in the army and the two spent most of the meal reminiscing. Gideon and Jack barely got the chance to contribute to the conversation, and instead, savored the fine cuts of steak on their plates.

The sheriff paid for all the meals before the men walked back to the stable. Scotty had switched their saddles to the rented horses and had the animals tied out front. After all the goodbyes were said, the three men rode off toward Junction City.

They hadn't traveled very far before Gideon realized that his horse had a bone-jarring trot. "I'd rather have

Rowdy taking a plug out of me every day than have to ride this thing. You could strap a churn on its back and have butter in no time."

"Mine rides good," Jack said. "I'll trade you for a while when you get tired."

"I'd have to let the stirrups down to ride your horse. I've been meaning to tell you that Chloe didn't even have to adjust them at all that day she rode with me," Gideon said.

"Gideon Johann, you are an insufferable man. Your ass can be bounced clear up to your shoulders for all I care."

The men rode most of the night at a steady trot, slowing to a walk occasionally to let the horses rest and to give themselves a break from posting. They would stop whenever they encountered a creek to water the animals. By the time the first light of the morning broke to the east, the men were so tired they could barely stay in the saddle. Jack managed to nap as they rode the last few miles before reaching the edge of Junction City. They arrived in front of the jail at seven-thirty in the morning.

Sheriff Whitney led the way into the office. The sheriff of Saline County sat at his desk, drinking coffee and reading the paper. He looked up and saw the three bedraggled men. Only their badges gave away that they were anything but drifters.

"You must be Sheriff Whitney. Good morning. Gentlemen, have yourself a seat. You all look as if you could use one. I'm Sheriff Isbell."

"Good to meet you," Sheriff Whitney said as he shook hands with the lawman.

Sheriff Isbell got up and grabbed some coffee cups. As he began pouring coffee, he said, "I hate to tell you this, but if your bank robbers rode into Junction City, they didn't come downtown."

Gideon and Jack slumped into a pair of chairs against the wall. As Sheriff Isbell passed out the coffees, Sheriff Whitney took a moment to process the news before taking a seat in front of the desk.

"That's sure not what I wanted to hear. I don't understand where they went," Sheriff Whitney said.

Sheriff Isbell sat back down at his desk. "I figure if they are here, they must know somebody and stayed with them. I have deputies on the northeast, east, and southeast sides of town to watch for them if they try to leave. They surely wouldn't change their general direction now."

"That's good thinking. I hate to imagine we rode all night and were given the slip."

"So tell me about this bank robbery," Sheriff Isbell said.

"It was pretty well thought out. They kidnapped the bank's vice president and forced him to open the vault after hours. They left him and his wife bound up. The only mistake they made was that a couple of the townsfolk saw them hanging around the bank. One of them has a scar across his chin and is stocky. The taller one has dark hair and always wears a black coat," Sheriff Whitney replied before sipping his coffee loudly.

The information caused Sheriff Isbell to purse his lips, look up at the ceiling, and rub his chin. "If your telegram hadn't said that the robbers were riding a bay and a dun, I would think you were describing the Carson brothers. A horse kicked Simon in the chin when he was a boy. They ride a buckskin and a chestnut. That's the only horses they own as far as I know except for a harness team."

"They were riding a buckskin and a chestnut. One of the horses went lame and they traded them in at Salina."

Sheriff Isbell rubbed his hand across his lips, looking as if he were deep in thought. "Those boys are cabinetmakers. They've never been in any trouble whatsoever. I just can't imagine it would be them."

"Have they been gone a few days?" Sheriff Whitney asked.

"Not that I know of. I know that their shop's been open, but I had no reason to go inside of it. They've been known to let their wives run it if they had to head to a sawmill somewhere to get lumber."

"I'd say we need to go have a talk with them and see their horses."

As Sheriff Isbell picked up his hat, he said, "I sure hope it's not them. They have families to feed. Maybe their business isn't doing as good as I thought it was."

"Do they know how to handle guns?"

"They both fought in the war so I would say so, but I think all they keep in the shop is a shotgun behind the counter."

The two sheriffs decided they would enter the cabinetmaking shop through the front and send Gideon and Jack to the rear to act as reinforcements in the event of trouble.

Sheriff Isbell led the way through the door. "Simon, Isaac, I need to talk to you boys," he called out.

The brothers were standing behind the cabinets they were busy sanding. They had arrived at the shop that morning with a bad case of the nerves, and decided to wear their revolvers. When they saw the sheriffs, they drew their guns, sending the lawmen diving to the floor behind a row of finished cabinets as the bullets tore through the front door.

At the sound of the shots, Gideon tried opening the back door and found it locked. He took his foot and kicked the door near the knob. The jamb gave way and the door flung open. Gideon and Jack rushed in, but the rear of the shop was stacked high with wood and cabinets. They could hear the gun battle in the front of the store, but their view was obscured by all the inventory. Jack went one direction and Gideon the other to try reaching the others.

Sheriff Isbell and Sheriff Whitney would pop up over the cabinets and take a shot at the brothers. Simon and Isaac were doing the same. The only casualties were the handcrafted cabinets.

The brothers decided to make a run for it, weaving their way through the maze of cabinets. They came around a corner and were standing face to face with Gideon. Without hesitating, Gideon began firing his revolver. The first two shots hit Isaac, sending him toppling over backwards.

Simon escaped down another aisle. When he turned towards the back of the building, he plowed into Jack, sending both men to the floor. Simon landed on the mountain man with all his weight, knocking the air out of him. As Jack struggled for air, Simon tried crawling away. Jack took his revolver and slammed it into Simon's head until the cabinetmaker collapsed on him again.

As Gideon chased after Simon, he heard the tussle and yelled, "Jack, I'm coming." He rounded the corner and nearly tripped over the men. In his excited state, he managed to fling the unconscious Simon to the side with one heave. Jack had his mouth wide open gasping for air like a fish tossed on the riverbank. Gideon looked his friend up and down for signs of blood. "Jack, what happened to you?"

Jack waved his hand in the air and shook his head.

After retrieving Simon's gun, Gideon yelled, "We got them."

Once Jack got air into his lungs, he said, "I got the air knocked out of me. I thought my eyes were going to pop out of my head."

"Well, you sure weren't a pretty sight. I'm liable to have nightmares over seeing you," Gideon said.

"You are a cold soul, Gideon Johann."

The sheriffs finally made their way through the maze to the deputies.

"I had to kill the other one," Gideon said.

Simon began stirring. He opened his eyes to see Sheriff Isbell pointing his revolver at him.

"Simon, what were you thinking? You just got your brother killed. You best tell me where the money is. The judge will go a lot easier on you if you do, and I heard tell that vigilantes in Ellsworth already strung up one man this year. I would imagine you might be the second if they don't get their money back," Sheriff Isbell said.

The cabinetmaker rubbed the knots on his head and groaned. "We were going broke. Look at all this inventory. Nobody is buying from us since that new shop opened up and started undercutting us."

"Where is the money?"

"It's under the floorboards."

"Show me."

Simon got to his feet unsteadily and wobbled toward the hideaway.

"You get back and let me open it," Sheriff Isbell ordered. "I don't want any surprises."

The sheriff used his knife to pry up the hatch in the floor. The money was still in the saddlebags used in the robbery.

"I'm sorry, sheriff," Simon said as he gazed at his feet.

"Me too, Simon. Let's head to the jail. You're going to have to get used to bars in your windows," the sheriff said.

Chapter 22

After Simon Carson was locked in a cell, Sheriff Whitney sent a telegram to Marshal Morco to let him know the money had been recovered. The men then went for breakfast. They were so exhausted that they had to concentrate to keep from staggering as they walked down the boardwalk, but their bellies were all growling so loudly that skipping a meal was not an option. Once they entered the diner, Sheriff Isbell hollered out to the cook to "Give them the works." The waitress brought out plates heaped with delicious smelling slices of ham, bacon, eggs, biscuits, and gravy. Not bothering to waste time on conversation, the group chowed into the tasty food with gusto.

When Sheriff Isbell finally set down his fork, he said, "I guess I better go tell the Carson brothers' wives the bad news. This certainly isn't how I planned my day. I still have a hard time imagining that a couple of cabinetmakers got it in their head to rob a bank. Here I thought we'd be arresting some famous outlaws before the day was through, and get our names in all the newspapers throughout the country."

"People can surprise you, that's for sure," Sheriff Whitney said before wiping his mouth with a napkin. "We'll be checking into the hotel. Maybe we'll see you tonight for dinner if we wake up."

Sheriff Whitney was so pleased to have the stolen money recovered that he sprang for separate rooms for each of them.

As they were walking up the stairway to their rooms, Gideon said, "I'm not sure I can sleep anymore without listening to your snoring."

Jack shook his head. "Well, I'm already practiced up today for putting people to sleep. I'll gladly lay my gun upside your head too if you want some help."

The men retired to their rooms and slept until dinnertime. Sheriff Isbell joined them for supper in the hotel dining room and then accompanied them to the Hideaway Saloon. They drank a couple of beers with the sheriff, but were still feeling exhausted, and returned early to the hotel to go to bed.

In the morning, Sheriff Whitney decided to give the horses another day of rest before heading back toward Ellsworth. He had breakfast with Gideon and Jack and then left to visit friends he had in Junction City.

With nothing to do, Gideon and Jack strolled down to the jail. Sheriff Isbell sat at his desk, drinking coffee and reading in the newspaper of his sensationalized exploits in yesterday's arrest of Simon Carson.

"Good morning, boys. Grab yourself some coffee," the sheriff said.

"Thank you," Gideon said as he headed for the coffee pot.

"I never got around to telling you two, but that was some fine work you did yesterday. If you ever need a job, come see me."

"We'll keep that in mind," Gideon said as he handed Jack a cup. He sat down beside him. "I wanted to ask you if you knew Martin Sanders."

Sheriff Isbell chuckled. "Did he end up in Ellsworth? How many times have you had to arrest him?"

"None. He works at the livery stable and hasn't caused any trouble that I know of," Gideon replied before taking a sip of coffee.

"Well, keep your eye on him. I've arrested that boy so many times I've lost count. He can pick a lock slicker than a whistle. He's just not very good at laying low afterward. I should have hauled him before the judge, but his momma is such a nice lady that I hated putting her through all that. She's been through enough in her life. I'd keep Martin a couple of days and turn him loose with a warning. The last time I arrested him I gave him a choice – get out of town or face the judge. That's the last I ever saw of him," Sheriff Isbell said.

"We'll keep an eye on him."

"Yeah, that's a sad story. The only mistake his momma, Kathleen, ever made was getting in a family way before she was married. The rumor had it that the daddy was a no-count by the name of Teddy Calhoun. I know it was true too because the minute Kathleen started showing, Teddy up and disappeared. I've never heard of him again. You could just look at Martin and see that he was Teddy's boy . . ."

Gideon slapped his leg. "That's it. I kept thinking I'd crossed paths with Martin in the past. That's why I asked about him, but it was his resemblance to Teddy. Teddy ran a saloon in Ellsworth and was murdered."

"Oh, that doesn't sound good," the sheriff said.

"We arrested a man for the murder. I had my doubts that Lonnie did it, but his alibi didn't hold up. We need to take a look at Martin."

"Has he been convicted?"

"No, the case hasn't come to trial yet."

"I never would peg Martin for murder, but he probably bears some resentment toward his pa for never being around for him. God knows that he and Kathleen lived hard lives without a man to support them."

"Thank you, sheriff. I think you just might have saved a man from being falsely convicted. I'm going to go send a telegram to the marshal in case the trial begins before we get back."

As Gideon and Jack walked toward the telegraph office, Jack said, "That was a keen eye you had. I never noticed the likeness between Teddy and Martin."

"I guess I didn't either. And it wasn't as if we were around Teddy very much. I just thought Martin looked familiar."

In the telegram, Gideon put that he had new reasons to believe in Lonnie's innocence. He didn't send any information about Martin, fearing the marshal would mishandle the situation without all the details.

After they left the telegraph office, Jack said, "Let's sit down on this here bench. I want to talk to you."

Gideon looked at his friend with a puzzled expression. "Sure."

"I needed to let you know that I'm ready to head back to the mountains. I'm starting to miss them something fierce, and I need to begin scouting out the beaver. This badge is getting heavy, if you know what I mean," Jack said as he sat.

"You don't owe me an explanation. I'm surprised you've stayed as long as you have," Gideon said.

"But are you going to be fine without me around to keep an eye on you?"

"Jack, I've been on my own for years. This is the life I chose. I do appreciate your looking out for me, but I'll be fine."

"But you were so troubled when we left Boulder that you had me worried about your well-being."

"I know I was, but I've been sleeping fine lately. Jack you're a mountain man. We're both loners. You need to get back to those mountains and quit worrying about me," Gideon urged.

"I must be getting sentimental in my old age. Maybe it's because you saved my life, but I feel responsible for you," Jack said as he leaned back against the bench.

"We are all squared up on looking out for each other. I've had enough of this subject," Gideon said as he pressed his hand against his chest and grimaced. "Those scabs on my chest are itching so badly that I swear I'd like to take a currycomb to them."

"You let them alone. I don't want to be nursemaiding you."

"I'm smart enough to know that. Doesn't mean I can't complain a little though."

"What are you going to do after I leave?" Jack asked.

"If George will have me, I think I'll stick to being a deputy until I feel the need to move on. I haven't been too impressed with those trail crews so far."

"What about Chloe?"

"I think we're fine. She understands things now," Gideon said.

"I still wish I could fix what's broken in you. Chloe could be a keeper."

"I know, Jack. Believe me, I know."

At supper that night, Gideon told Sheriff Whitney the news he had learned about Martin Sanders. The sheriff contorted his face all up and he tried to recall a resemblance between Teddy and his son. He finally gave up and stated that he would take Gideon and Sheriff Isbell's word on the father and son's likeness.

That night when Gideon went to bed, as soon as he closed his eyes he had the vision of the little boy staring at him. It seemed as if mentioning earlier in day that he'd been sleeping better had brought the child charging back into his life. Gideon tried to fall asleep for close to an hour before getting up and walking to the saloon. He bought a bottle of whiskey and returned to his room. A third of a bottle later, he fell asleep.

After breakfast the next morning, the Ellsworth lawmen left with their prisoner and the stolen money. They made it to Salinas by suppertime. Marshal Leinberger locked Simon in his jail and dined with the men. The marshal showed curiosity about the capture of Simon, and the sheriff gladly recounted the events as if the gunfight was one of the greatest shootouts in the history of the west. Afterward, Marshal Leinberger accompanied them to the saloon and the men drank a couple of beers with him before retiring to their rooms, tired from the day of riding.

The visions haunted Gideon again that night. He sat up in bed and rubbed his hand through his shock of hair, worried that the boy was back again for good. His saddlebag sat beside the bed and Gideon pulled out the whiskey bottle. He took two long drinks and fell back into the bed. Sleep eventually came sometime during the night.

Scotty, the blacksmith, had their own horses ready for them the next day when the lawmen headed to the livery stable after breakfast. Sheriff Whitney paid the bill and they gladly departed for Ellsworth.

"I'm never going to complain about Rowdy again for as long as I live. This horse feels like sitting on a big stuffed couch compared to that thing I rode yesterday," Gideon said after traveling a couple of miles.

"I'll bet you ten dollars that'll go out the window the next time he takes a plug out of you," Jack said.

"I thought mountain men didn't like to talk much and preferred their own company," Gideon said.

"Not when I get to see a clown like you."

They reached Ellsworth late in the afternoon. Marshal Morco wasn't in the jail when they arrived. After Sheriff Whitney locked Simon in a cell, he ordered Gideon and Jack to go home, telling Gideon he could tell the marshal about Martin in the morning.

Gideon and Jack wasted no time in riding their horses to the livery stable. As they dismounted, Martin came out to get their mounts. The boy appeared cheerful, asking whether they had captured the bank robbers. Gideon told him that they had, but provided no details.

As they walked toward George's home, Gideon said, "I kind of feel sorry for Martin. He's never had much of a chance in life, and tomorrow, I expect we'll be arresting him for murder. Doesn't hardly seem fair."

"It is sad, but he made his choice. At least he ruined his life with an intentional act instead of eating himself up with guilt for something he did by accident," Jack said as he gazed at Gideon.

Gideon smiled sadly and shook his head, wishing he had a good reply for Jack.

Chapter 23

On the morning after returning to Ellsworth, Gideon and Jack showed up early at the jail. Gideon quickly came to the conclusion that Marshal Morco was as nosy as a little old man waiting his turn for a haircut in a barbershop. The marshal insisted that both of his deputies recount the shootout in the cabinet shop even though Sheriff Whitney had already told him all about it the previous evening. He couldn't get enough details to satisfy his inquisitiveness and asked questions until the subject was finally exhausted.

After rolling a cigarette with fingers permanently stained with tobacco, the marshal lit it and took a puff. He looked at Gideon and his smile faded away. "Sheriff Whitney said I needed to talk to you about this nonsense that Lonnie is innocent. What's on your mind?"

Gideon told the marshal all he had learned from Sheriff Isbell.

The marshal twisted his mouth and scratched his cheek before taking another puff on his cigarette. "I have to admit that little shit does look like Teddy now that you mention it. Sounds like he has motive, too."

"That it does, and I'm pretty sure that Phillip Tyrone and Lisa Young lied about what really happened that night."

"So how do you propose we prove Martin is the murderer?" the marshal asked.

"I think we should ask Mr. Nance for permission to search the room Martin lives in at the stable. Mr. Nance owns the property and has the right to give us access. You can search the room for Teddy's pocket watch and anything else you may find that points to his guilt. Jack and I will keep an eye on Martin," Gideon replied.

"Don't you want to be the one that goes in to try to solve this crime?"

"Nah, if we're right about this, nobody has to know all the details on how we finally solved the murder. Maybe it will put a feather in your cap with the mayor if you get all the credit."

Marshal Morco chuckled. "I don't know about that after arresting three people before I finally got the right one. A shotgun approach to the law is not a good thing. Let's get this over with."

The marshal put his hat on and led the way to the livery stable.

Martin came out to meet the lawmen. "Do you fellows need your horses?" he asked.

"No, we need to talk to Mr. Nance," Marshal Morco answered.

"He's in his office."

The livery stable owner, sensing that this was no ordinary visit, eyed the lawmen apprehensively when they walked into his office. "What can I do for you men?" he asked.

Marshal Morco explained the situation and asked for permission to search Martin's room.

Mr. Nance rubbed his forehead and leaned back in his chair. "I hope this isn't true. Martin's not a bad young man at all, but do what you have to do."

The marshal and Mr. Nance went to the room while Gideon and Jack walked over to where Martin stood feeding horses.

"What's going on?" Martin asked.

"You just need to stay here with us," Gideon said.

Martin looked warily toward his room and started shifting his weight from one foot to the other. As he rubbed the back of his neck, the tightness in his chest made his breath sound ragged.

A few minutes later, Marshal Morco emerged from the room swinging a pocket watch by its chain and holding up a skeleton key in his other hand. "Martin, what do you have to say for yourself?" he asked.

The sight of the evidence caused Martin to make a sound like all of the air had been crushed from his lungs. He flung himself onto the ground and pounded the dirt with his fists like a toddler throwing a tantrum. "No. No. No," he screamed hysterically. "This can't be happening. That son of a bitch ruined my and my momma's lives. When I found out that my pa lived here in town, I went and introduced myself to him. Do you know what he said to me? He told me to get the hell out of his saloon and that he never wanted to see me again. He couldn't even be civil to his own son. I snuck in the saloon and killed him. This bastard child killed that lowlife bastard. And I'd do it all over again if given the chance."

Gideon and Jack exchanged glances, shaking their heads sadly at the turn of events. While both had expected the outcome, the reasons for the murder and the fact they were arresting one so young, made the whole ordeal all the sadder. As they leaned down, each grabbed one of Martin's arms. They pulled him to his feet and began the trek back to the jail. The marshal followed behind with the evidence. Once they were back in the jail, Martin was locked in the cell beside of

Lonnie. The saloonkeeper watched with an air of indifference brought on by the burden of fearing he'd soon be convicted of a crime he did not commit.

Marshal Morco took the key from Gideon and unlocked Lonnie's cell. "Lonnie, I owe you an apology. I now know that you are innocent. We just arrested the real killer. I hope you can find it in your heart to forgive me, and that your business will not suffer too badly."

Lonnie looked up skeptically at the three law officers standing in front of his cell as if he wondered if they were trying to trick him. "I'm free to go?" he asked.

"Yes, you are, and I promise to be your first customer when you open your doors back up," Marshal Morco said.

"Why did Martin kill him?" Lonnie asked as he looked over at the young man.

"Teddy was his pa and he didn't do right by him."

With a shake of his head, Lonnie got to his feet. As he stepped out of the cell, he turned toward Gideon. He pointed his finger in Gideon's face and yelled, "This is all your damn fault. I'm liable to lose my saloon because of you. I told you the truth and you took the word of others that had something to hide."

Jack pounced like a cat going after a mouse. He grabbed Lonnie by the throat and pinned him against the cell bars. "Gideon was the one that never gave up on you. If not for him, you'd be going to trial. You should be thanking him instead of placing blame where it doesn't belong," he yelled out before releasing his grip.

Lonnie's eyes were watering as he rubbed his throat and his voice came out raspy. "I'm sorry. I didn't know. I guess I should have asked questions instead of assuming the worst. To show there are no hard feelings, you all come by the saloon when I get it open and I'll buy you a beer," he said before making a hasty exit from the jail.

After the men returned to the office area and took seats, Jack said, "Marshal, today is my last day. I'm headed back to Boulder tomorrow. All this walking around on flat ground is starting to make me feel lopsided. I need my mountains."

Marshal Morco rubbed his head as he gathered his thoughts. "I know you've stayed longer than you intended. You've been a good deputy and I appreciate the work you've done here. I wish you well," he said.

Gideon pulled off his hat and rubbed his scar. "Today is my last day, too."

Jack let his mouth drop open in shock as he looked over at Gideon.

The marshal pulled his head back and braced his hands against his desk. "What? Have you already found a trail crew to your liking? Most of them aren't even ready to head back yet."

"No, it's just time for me to move on. I've enjoyed my time working for you, but I'm a drifter at heart."

Marshal Morco slapped his desk. "Well, you two sure know how to ruin a day that started off real promising. I wish you both the best. The other deputies resent how you two have become my favorites anyway. I guess I'll have to kiss up to them to get back in their good graces. You boys go on and get out of here. Go do what you need to do to get ready for your travels.

Outside of the jail, Jack asked, "Are you headed back to Boulder with me?"

"Nah, Jack, you know I don't ever backtrack," Gideon replied.

"Then why are you leaving now?"

"Ever since I told you that I was sleeping good, well, since then things have been bad. I've drank almost a whole bottle of whiskey in the last three days to get to sleep. Just like I knew it was time to leave Boulder, it's time to leave Ellsworth."

"Where are you going?"

"I don't have a clue. I guess whichever way the wind blows me," Gideon said, forcing a grin.

Jack adjusted his hat. "I'd give my eyeteeth to fix what ails you."

"I'd let you if I thought it would do the trick. Let's go lay in some supplies and start saying our goodbyes," Gideon said with a nod of his head.

Chapter 24

The news of Gideon and Jack's impending departures caught George totally off guard. He'd known all along that neither man would be staying forever, but hadn't counted on having the news sprung on him at the last moment. Over the course of their stay, he had gotten so used to having Gideon and Jack in his house that he knew that the silence after their leaving would drive him crazy. As he fixed their final breakfast in his home, he moped around the kitchen and barely contributed to the conversation.

Jack watched his brother stirring eggs, noticing the slumped shoulders and hanging head. "George, come spring, I want you to take the train to Denver. From there, you can ride a stagecoach into Boulder. I want to show you the mountains. Boulder is a nice town and it's growing. You might even think about pulling up stakes and starting over there. We don't have a milliner. You'd have a monopoly on the hatmaking business."

George smiled and his eyes lit up at the invitation. "Thank you, Jack. I'd love to come see you. I don't know about moving. I'm kind of used to Ellsworth, but I guess we can see how I like the town."

"You just write me a letter when you're coming. I usually make it out of the mountains and back into town sometime in April."

Gideon watched the brothers' interactions with amusement. He'd never been convinced that their relationship had been as strained as Jack had made things sound, but if it were true, those feelings certainly no longer existed. Even though Jack would never admit it in a million years, the mountain man would miss being around his brother. "I can step outside when you two kiss goodbye," he said to rile Jack.

"Oh, you think you're such a funny man. If I knew what I know now, I probably would have just stood up and let them kill me on the day you saved my ass just to spare me your company," Jack said.

With a chortle, Gideon said, "George, I do want to thank you for your hospitality. I've enjoyed staying here with you, and I'll miss you fixing us breakfast every morning. A man could get used to that."

George's demeanor improved considerably with Jack's invitation and Gideon's compliment. He stood with his back straight and grinned. As he carried the food to the table, he said, "Well, I ain't afraid to say that I'm going to miss having you two in my house. It'll be mighty quiet around here."

The men had a lively meal with lots of ribbing of each other in an attempt to ignore the parting about to come.

When the food was all consumed, Jack let out a sigh and stood. He held out his hand and shook with George. "Promise me that I'll see you in the spring."

"You have my word. God's speed. Don't freeze to death in those mountains of yours," George said.

Gideon shook hands with George. "Thanks again. You take care of yourself. I'm liable to look you up when I wear out this here hat. I'm right fond of it."

"I'm sure I'll still be making them. It's the only thing I'm good at anyway. You be careful in your travels, Gideon," George said.

After gathering up their meager possession, Gideon and Jack said one last goodbye to George before leaving.

The two men walked to the livery stable in silence, contemplating saying goodbye, and going their separate ways.

In front of the stable, Gideon held out his hand. "Jack, I'm going to miss you. You're the only buddy I've had since the war. You take care of yourself. I guess this is it. I don't suppose we'll ever meet again so don't forget about me. Goodbye, my friend."

Jack wouldn't release Gideon's hand. He held it with a firm grasp as he looked Gideon in the eyes. "We've had some memorable times in the short period we've known each other – that's for sure. You're still a young man, but when you get older, you are going to realize that this world is a lot smaller than you think now. I just have a notion that we'll meet up again someday. In fact, I believe the next time I see you that you'll be a happily married man."

With a chuckle, Gideon said, "Now you're sounding like a crazy old mountain man that's spent too much time living alone. Take care of yourself. You are certainly one of a kind. Goodbye, Jack."

"You laugh at me all you want, but just now, I got this feeling that better days are ahead for you. Until we meet again, Gideon Johann, you take care of yourself," Jack said. He turned quickly toward the livery stable and marched away. His eyes were getting misty, and he wasn't about to let Gideon see him get sentimental. He began getting riled up at the notion that a loner like himself could get emotional over leaving behind his brother and his friend. To his way of thinking, Farting Jack Dolan needed some time alone in the mountains to get back to being his hermit self.

Gideon walked over toward the general store. He had already told Chloe that he was leaving and had promised to come by before departing. The place was bustling with customers, but when Sean saw Gideon, he made eye contact with his daughter and nodded his head toward the back of the store. Without wasting a moment, Chloe headed to the back and out into the alley with Gideon following right behind her.

"So you're really leaving?" Chloe asked as she turned to face Gideon.

"I have to go. I really planned on staying for a while, but things have changed. I know when it's time to move on," Gideon replied.

Chloe looked Gideon in the eyes for a moment before speaking. Realizing that she would never see him again, she tried to drink in all of his features, especially his deep blue eyes. "You know that you could have a really nice life here if you wanted, but you'd rather run around all over the country being miserable."

"Chloe, that is not true. This certainly is not the life I ever envisioned for myself way back when. If I told you to stop missing your momma, could you just up and quit?" Gideon asked.

"Well, of course not. What kind of silly question is that?"

"Because it is the same thing with me. You can't just tell me to quit feeling guilty about my past and expect me to magically change. Believe me, I wish it were so simple, but it's not. Please try to understand," Gideon pleaded.

Tears began puddling in Chloe's eyes, and she squeezed them and her mouth tightly shut. She felt embarrassed and threw herself into Gideon's arms so he couldn't see her face. "Damn you, Gideon Johann. I'm going to miss you. If I end up an old maid, I'm going to blame you," she said, laughing as she cried.

"You're not going to end up an old maid. You'll find the right man and have those children you always dreamed of raising. You'll be glad I got away," Gideon said as he patted her back.

"I'm going to miss you."

"I'll miss you, too," Gideon said. He bent his head down and kissed Chloe. Their lips lingered for a moment before Gideon abruptly broke away. "Goodbye, Chloe."

"Goodbye, Gideon."

Gideon turned and walked down the alley without looking back. After retrieving Rowdy from the livery stable, he rode away at a lope. He didn't have a clue as to where he was headed, but as long as he could outrun his demons for a while, he didn't care. He swore aloud that he would never put himself or another woman through what he had just done with Chloe. As Gideon looked over his shoulder at the town growing distant in his view, he wondered how many more places he had yet to travel to before his running days were done. He figured he wouldn't have the final tally until he took his last breath.

About the Author

Duane Boehm is a musician, songwriter, and author. He lives on a mini-farm with his wife and an assortment of dogs. Having written short stories throughout his lifetime, he shared them with friends and with their encouragement began his journey as a novelist. Please feel free to email him at boehmduane@gmail.com or like his Facebook Page www.facebook.com/DuaneBoehmAuthor.